He wanted her as much as she wanted him. Elizabeth thought she must have died and gone to heaven

He tasted her with his lips and his tongue, and when she arched her back, he groaned, a deep, dark, sensual sound that sent a thrill coursing through her veins.

She plowed her fingers through Cullen's hair, holding him close, thinking to herself, *I always wanted my first time to be with you.*

Cullen lifted his head. She went still. Surely she hadn't said that aloud. Had she?

"This is your first time?" He sounded almost angry.

"That can't come as much of a surprise," she whispered. "But it doesn't change anything."

Cullen pulled back, resting on his knees. "It changes everything."

Dear Harlequin Intrigue Reader,

Cupid's bow is loaded at Harlequin Intrigue with four fabulous stories of breathtaking romantic suspense—starting with the continuation of Cassie Miles's COLORADO SEARCH AND RESCUE miniseries. In *Wedding Captives*, lovers reunite on a mountaintop... unfortunately they're also snowbound with a madman!

And there's no better month to launch our new modern gothic continuity series MORIAH'S LANDING. Amanda Stevens emerges from the New England fog with *Secret Sanctuary*, the first of four titles coming out over the next several months. You can expect all of the classic themes you love in these stories, plus more of the contemporary edge you've come to expect from our brand of romantic suspense.

You know what can happen *In the Blink of an Eye...?* Julie Miller does! And you can find out, too, in the next installment of her TAYLOR CLAN series.

Finally, Jean Barrett takes you to New Orleans for some *Private Investigations* with battling P.I.'s. It's a regular showdown in the French Quarter—where absolutely anything goes.

So celebrate Valentine's Day with the most confounding mystery of all...that of the heart.

Deep, rich chocolate wishes,

Denise O'Sullivan
Associate Senior Editor
Harlequin Intrigue

SECRET SANCTUARY

AMANDA STEVENS

HARLEQUIN®

TORONTO • NEW YORK • LONDON
AMSTERDAM • PARIS • SYDNEY • HAMBURG
STOCKHOLM • ATHENS • TOKYO • MILAN • MADRID
PRAGUE • WARSAW • BUDAPEST • AUCKLAND

Special thanks and acknowledgment
are given to Amanda Stevens for her contribution
to the MORIAH'S LANDING series.

ISBN 0-373-22650-0

SECRET SANCTUARY

Visit us at www.eHarlequin.com

Printed in U.S.A.

ABOUT THE AUTHOR

Born and raised in a small, Southern town, Amanda Stevens frequently draws on memories of her birthplace to create atmospheric settings and casts of eccentric characters. She is the author of over twenty-five novels, the recipient of a Career Achievement Award for Romantic/Mystery, and a 1999 RITA Award finalist in the Gothic/Romantic Suspense category. She now resides in Texas with her husband, teenage twins and her cat, Jesse, who also makes frequent appearances in her books.

Books by Amanda Stevens

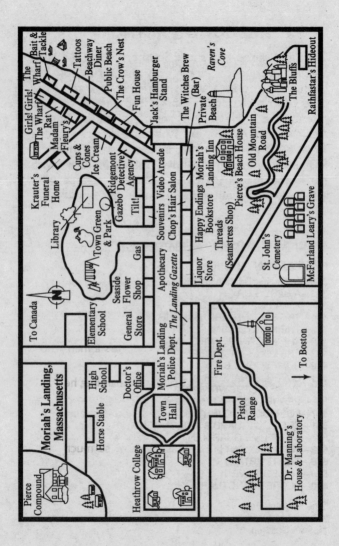

Moriah's Landing, Massachusetts

Pierce Compound

Heathrow College

High School

Horse Stable

Doctor's Office

Town Hall

Moriah's Landing Police Dept.

The Landing Gazette

Fire Dept.

Pistol Range

Dr. Manning's House & Laboratory

To Boston

To Canada

N

Elementary School

General Store

Seaside Flower Shop

Gas

Apothecary

Library

Town Green & Park

Krauter's Funeral Home

Cups & Cones Ice Cream

Madam Fleury's

Rat's

The Wharf

Girls! Girls!

The Wharf

Bait & Tackle

Tattoos

Beachway Diner

Public Beach

The Crow's Nest

Fun House

Jack's Hamburger Stand

Ridgemont Detective Agency

Gazebo

Tilt!

Souvenirs

Video Arcade

Chop's Hair Salon

Happy Endings Bookstore

Threads (Seamstress Shop)

Moriah's Landing Inn

Pierce's Beach House

The Witches Brew (Bar)

Private Beach

Raven's Cove

Old Mountain Road

The Bluffs

Rathfastar's Hideout

St. John's Cemetery

McFarland Leary's Grave

Liquor Store

CAST OF CHARACTERS

Elizabeth Douglas—An expert in criminology, she's standing in the way of a killer's ultimate revenge.

Detective Cullen Ryan—A man with a dark past of his own. He vows to protect Elizabeth from the killer, but can he protect her from himself?

Professor Lucian LeCroix—He arrived in Moriah's Landing on the night the first body was discovered.

Dr. Paul Fortier—He has an eye for the ladies—especially his students.

Dr. Leland Manning—A pioneer in gene therapy research. What, exactly, is the nature of the experiments he conducts at his isolated compound?

David Bryson—A recluse, he was a suspect twenty years ago in the killings that terrorized Moriah's Landing. Has his grief for a lost love driven him to do unspeakable evil?

Ned Krauter—The town mortician, he's a man who enjoys his work.

Dr. René Rathfaster—A brilliant researcher, he disappeared several years ago when allegations surfaced that he conducted genetic experiments on human test subjects.

Geoffrey Pierce—How does he know so much about serial killers?

This book is gratefully dedicated to B.J. Daniels,
Dani Sinclair and Joanna Wayne,
my partners in crime as well as my friends.

Prologue

The sky had been clear all day, but as evening fell, storm clouds moved in from the sea, blocking fragile moonlight and deepening shadows across a bleak and eerie landscape. The wind had picked up, too, stirring dead leaves over the necropolis.

There was something in that wind, Elizabeth Douglas thought with a shiver. Something evil.

She glanced at the luminous dial on her watch. Almost midnight. Time for the ghosts to rise....

She and her friends huddled just inside the cemetery walls as they gazed in trepidation at the shadowy formation of headstones and crumbling mausoleums. Silhouetted against the darkness, marble angels stood with bowed heads and furled wings, celestial sentinels as cold and silent as the graves they watched over.

Elizabeth didn't want to be here. She wanted to be anywhere *but* here. Spending the night in St. John's Cemetery as part of a sorority initiation was just plain crazy, not to mention against the rules. They'd all be in big trouble if the school got wind of what they were doing.

"Do you think we'll see Leary's ghost tonight?" Claire Cavendish asked nervously. A pale, slender girl, she was even more skittish about the coming night than Elizabeth. Claire jumped as the heavy, iron gates clanged shut behind them in the wind. "They say he rises every five years."

"Oh, come on," Kat Ridgemont scoffed. "You don't really believe all those stories about ghosts and witches, do you? That stuff was made up just to attract tourists. None of it's true."

"What about those women who were murdered in Moriah's Landing fifteen years ago?" Claire challenged. "Did they make that up, too?"

"Claire!" Brie Dudley warned in a low voice.

Claire clapped a hand to her mouth. "Oh, God, Kat. I'm so sorry. I forgot."

Kat shrugged. "It's okay. I forget sometimes myself."

But Elizabeth didn't think that was true. Kat's mother was thought to be the first victim of a serial killer who had terrorized Moriah's Landing fifteen years ago. Before his gruesome reign ended, three more young women had lost their lives, and Elizabeth knew that in spite of what Kat said, her mother's death still haunted her. The killings haunted the entire town because the murderer had never been caught.

Gooseflesh prickled the back of Elizabeth's neck. She fervently wanted to believe they had nothing to fear tonight—from the killer or from Leary's ghost—but she couldn't seem to shake her disquiet.

But at fifteen, she was the baby of the group. The other girls were 18, and Elizabeth was always conscious of the age difference. She wasn't about to be the first to suggest they turn back.

"Elizabeth?"

She blinked as the beam of someone's flashlight caught her in the face.

"You okay?" Brie asked worriedly. "You're being awfully quiet. You haven't said a word since we got here."

Elizabeth shrugged. "I've just been thinking."

Kat glanced over her shoulder. "About McFarland Leary?" she teased.

"Who else?" Elizabeth tried to say lightly, but her tone sounded a bit defensive even to her.

"You believe in ghosts, too, don't you?" Claire whispered beside her.

Elizabeth hesitated. She wasn't sure what she believed in. She just knew there were things in this world that couldn't be explained.

"Look!" Tasha Pierce said on a breathless whisper. "There it is!"

Tasha and Kat were in front, and they came to a stop as Tasha angled her light over Leary's grave. Weather and time had worn smooth the face of the headstone, until all but a faint trace of carving remained. But they knew it was Leary's grave.

Lightning flickered overhead as wind gusted through the cemetery. Shivering, Tasha tucked her blond hair inside her collar. "We'd better get started before the storm hits."

The girls dropped to their knees, forming a circle around the grave. Tasha placed her flashlight in the center, then removed an ornate wooden box from her backpack and held it up to the light.

"Inside are five scrolls," she intoned solemnly, her voice rising over the wind. "All but one are blank. Whosoever chooses the image of McFarland Leary must enter the haunted mausoleum. Alone."

Elizabeth was the last to draw. The others had waited for her, and now they all unrolled the tiny scrolls they'd each selected.

Beside her, Claire gave a horrified gasp. She held up the slip of paper so that everyone could see the etching of McFarland Leary.

Of all the girls, Claire was the least prepared to enter the haunted crypt alone. She was the most sensitive, the most easily frightened.

Elizabeth swallowed back her own fear. "I'll go in your place, Claire."

"No," Brie said. "You're the youngest, Elizabeth. I'm not letting you go anywhere alone. I'll go."

"I will." Tasha wadded up her scroll and stuffed it in her pocket. "This graveyard is full of Pierces. They'll protect one of their own."

"I say none of us go." Kat slammed the box shut and glanced around the circle. The wind whipped her black hair straight back from her face, making her look almost otherworldly. "They can't make us do this. Hazing went out with the Dark Ages."

There were murmurs of assent all around, but Claire shook her head and got to her feet. "It's not really hazing. Not the bad kind anyway. It's a tradition, and besides, I don't want to be the cause of any of us getting blackballed."

Kat scowled. "Who gives a flying—"

"I care," Claire said softly. "I can do this. I *need* to do this. I'll be fine."

Ignoring their protests, she picked up her flashlight and headed toward the ancient, crumbling mausoleum. In the intermittent flickers of lightning, Elizabeth could see a broken cross silhouetted against the stormy sky.

Slowly, Claire climbed the stone steps, opened the door, and then, glancing back only once, stepped through the dark portal. For a moment, they could see her light playing off the walls, and then the door creaked shut behind her.

"I'm going in there with her." Kat started to get to her feet, but Tasha grabbed her hand.

"No, wait. Maybe this really is something she wants to do on her own. Besides, we'll be right here if she needs us."

"Then we have to do our part," Brie said. "Are we all agreed?"

"Agreed," Elizabeth murmured, but guilt washed over her because as frightened as she was for Claire, a part of her was glad she wasn't the one inside that crypt.

"Once we join hands, the circle must not be broken," Tasha warned. "Physically or mentally."

Elizabeth squeezed her eyes closed as the girls joined hands, forming a protective circle as they summoned the natural forces of earth, air, fire and water to guard Claire from the ghosts of McFarland Leary and any other evil creatures who might roam the night.

But for just a split second, Elizabeth's mind wandered, and she thought about Cullen Ryan, a boy she'd had a crush on for ages. In trouble with the law, he'd dropped out of high school the year before and left town in the middle of the night. Elizabeth had no idea where he'd gone, or if she would ever see him again. But she prayed that wherever he was, he was safe, too.

And at the very moment when her concentration was weakened, when the spiritual circle was broken, thunder cracked overhead and a scream ripped through the darkness.

Claire!

The girls scrambled to their feet and raced toward the mausoleum. The door was stuck at first, but Kat managed to shove it open. The beam of her flashlight chased away shadows and shimmered off cobwebs suspended from the ornate ceiling. The scent of death and decay permeated the air, but there was no sign of Claire.

Elizabeth's heart started to pound with a terrible fear, a horrible premonition. She knew what had happened. While she'd been thinking about Cullen, the protective circle had been broken. The evil had been allowed in, and now Claire was gone.

And it was all Elizabeth's fault.

Chapter One

Five years later...

Elizabeth peered through her rain-spattered windshield as she wended her way around the curving drive toward the lighted mansion. February-bare oaks reached skeletal arms across the narrow lane, entwining with one another to form a natural arbor through which only thin tendrils of light could creep. The night was very dark.

Comprising well over a hundred acres of landscaped grounds, the Pierce compound—hidden from prying eyes by eight-foot, ivy-covered stone walls and thick stands of evergreens—was a masterpiece of design and privacy. The focal point was a lavish brick colonial owned by William and Maureen Pierce, the town's most prominent citizens.

A Pierce ancestor had founded Moriah's Landing in 1652, and the descendants had lived there ever since. The family remained active in many areas, most notably politics and science. Rumor had it that William and Maureen's lavish masquerade ball tonight was not only to continue the celebration that had begun on New Year's Eve to commemorate the

350th anniversary of the town's founding, but to help launch their eldest son's first political campaign.

Elizabeth liked Drew Pierce well enough and she thought he'd make a fine mayor, especially considering she didn't particularly care for the current one, Fredrick Thane. But in spite of the gossip regarding Drew and the potential for fireworks when Mayor Thane made his appearance at the ball, Elizabeth wasn't looking forward to this night. She'd never been particularly adept at socializing, and a masked ball was a little out of her league.

But then, disguising herself as someone other than who she truly was might not be such a bad thing, she decided. A seventeenth-century noblewoman, dressed to kill in a lavish gold ball gown with a plunging neckline, might know how to seize the moment—should one present itself—as Elizabeth Douglas never had.

She tugged at that neckline, discomfited by the amount of cleavage showing. Her new WonderBra, she decided, was truly that.

A bolt of lightning temporarily blinded her, and she slowed the car. Dark, roiling clouds hung low on the horizon, and over the sound of her car engine, she could hear the ominous rumble of thunder.

Earlier, when the first raindrops had pelted the roof of her cozy cottage, she'd hurried over to the window to stare out, thinking with a fatalistic shrug that, naturally, it would storm tonight. It always stormed in Moriah's Landing on momentous occasions—such as, she'd been told, on the night twenty years ago when Kat Ridgemont's mother had been murdered. And fifteen years later, on the night Claire Cavendish had vanished from the old haunted mausoleum.

Claire had been found in the cemetery several days later, her body tortured, her mind so tormented she hadn't been able to tell anyone what had happened to her. She'd resided ever since in a mental hospital a hundred miles west of Moriah's Landing, and every time Elizabeth drove up to visit her friend, she was stricken with guilt.

Which wasn't rational, she knew. There was nothing she could have done to save Claire that night. She and the other girls had never even seen who took Claire. To this day, the authorities still didn't know how the assailant had managed to get inside that mausoleum, subdue Claire and carry her off without anyone having seen anything.

At first, the girls had been under a cloud of suspicion—a sorority initiation ceremony gone terribly awry. But they were all so distraught, so terrified that the police had finally believed their wild tale.

To think that any of them would have done such a horrible thing to poor Claire....

Rounding a sharp curve, Elizabeth was momentarily facing eastward, and in the distance, she caught a glimpse of the Bluffs, a towering stone castle perched on the edge of a steep cliff that fell sharply away to the sea. It was there, on the jagged rocks below the castle, that Tasha Pierce had met with a horrible fate of her own, only one month after Claire had been found. It had been storming that night, too.

First Claire and then Tasha.

There were only three of them left, Elizabeth thought. She, Kat and Brie. And poor Brie hadn't exactly led a charmed life. She'd had to drop out of college after becoming pregnant, and she'd struggled ever since to take care of her fatherless child and her ill mother.

Elizabeth frowned. Sometimes she couldn't help wondering if they'd unleashed something terrible that night. Something evil. Sometimes she wondered if she and Kat would be next.

But then, Kat had already suffered. Her mother had been murdered when Kat was only three years old, and the killer had never been apprehended.

That left only Elizabeth.

As lightning fired the eastern sky, the castle came into sharp relief for just a split second. It was miles away, but Elizabeth could have sworn she saw a dark figure lurking on one of the turrets.

David Bryson, she thought with a shiver. The man who might or might not have killed her friend, Tasha.

Pulling up in front of the Pierce mansion, Elizabeth waited as two valets came rushing toward the car to meet her. One carried an umbrella which he used to shield her from the rain when she stepped outside, and the other climbed behind the wheel to park her new Audi. Elizabeth winced as the tires squealed against the wet pavement, but to her credit, she didn't look back. Instead, she wrapped her velvet cloak more tightly around her as she hurried up the granite steps.

As if of their own accord, the massive oak doors swung open, and Elizabeth stepped inside. Her cloak was removed from her shoulders, and she took a moment to arrange the shimmering folds of her gown. When she glanced up, she caught her breath.

She'd been to the mansion before, but it had been a long time ago, before Tasha's death, and Elizabeth had forgotten the elegance of the place, the sheer opulence.

A set of inlaid marble steps led down to an immense, sunken hall with a chessboard floor of black and white. Directly across the foyer, a magnificent staircase was crowned by a ten-foot cathedral window through which sunshine would pour in the daytime. Tonight, however, lightning flickered through dark clouds as rain slashed against the glass.

Below the window, the staircase split, curving gracefully on either side of the landing to a spacious gallery, brilliantly illuminated by crystal chandeliers and wall sconces that danced like candlelight.

To the left of the foyer, another set of double doors opened into a ballroom, and Elizabeth glimpsed the dazzling swish of costumes as swaying bodies seemed to float over the dance floor.

It was like stepping back in time. The women were adorned in glittering jewels and swirling silk ball gowns from another era, another century, while the men were festooned in everything from military uniforms to brocade breeches and powdered wigs.

And the flowers! Every hothouse from Moriah's Landing to Boston must have been emptied to accommodate such glorious arrangements, most of them done in red and white in honor of St. Valentine's Day, although the celebration had very little to do with the holiday. Red and pink cyclamens hovered like butterflies around a colored fountain that had been set up near the buffet tables, and heart-shaped candles floated in the water among fragrant rose petals and gardenia blossoms.

A more romantic setting, Elizabeth couldn't imagine, and here she was, dateless as usual.

As she lingered in the hall, reluctant to join the throng, a woman dressed in a gorgeous blue gown and an elaborate mask of peacock feathers drifted out of the ballroom toward her. The woman lowered the mask, and Elizabeth smiled, happy to see a friendly face.

Although she didn't know Rebecca Smith all that well, the two had hit it off when Elizabeth had gone into Threads, a design shop in town that Becca managed, looking for her costume. Becca had gently but firmly steered her away from the more austere designs that Elizabeth had automatically gravitated to and talked her into a golden fantasy concoction with a tight-fitting bodice that laced up the back and a skirt that swirled about her ankles when she walked.

Elizabeth raised her own swan-like mask to her face and pirouetted for Becca. ''Well,'' she said. ''How do I look?''

''Breathtaking,'' a male voice said behind her.

Elizabeth whirled, her gaze going immediately to the man who stood at the top of the entryway steps. He'd just come in from the rain, and the shoulders of his black cape glistened with moisture. He shrugged out of the heavy mantle, handing it to the butler without a glance, his gaze never wavering from the two women who stood below him in the foyer. He was dressed all in black, like a phantom, and the golden mask that covered one side of his face was at once hideous and beautiful.

As he slowly descended the stairs, Elizabeth had to fight the urge to step back from him. There was something about him...

''My name is Lucian LeCroix,'' he said in a voice as dark and liquid as the night. Before Elizabeth had time to catch her breath, he took her hand and lifted it to his lips.

"Pr-professor LeCroix?" she finally managed to stammer.

The brow on the unmasked side of his face lifted. "Why, yes. Don't tell me we've met. I'm certain I would have remembered."

"No, we've never met," Elizabeth acknowledged. "But I knew you were coming. We've been expecting you."

The brow lifted again. "We?"

"The staff at Heathrow College. You've come to replace Dr. Vintner, correct?" Ernst Vintner, the chairman of the English Department, had died suddenly from a massive coronary a few weeks ago. Instead of promoting one of his own tenured professors, Dr. Barloft, the college president, had hired the protégé of an old family friend. Professor LeCroix came with impeccable credentials, but Elizabeth couldn't help feeling a measure of resentment. She had friends among the faculty who should have had that position.

Professor LeCroix was still holding her hand, and Elizabeth pulled it away. She lifted her chin slightly. "My name is Elizabeth Douglas. I teach courses in criminology at Heathrow."

"*Dr.* Douglas," Becca said.

If he was surprised by Elizabeth's title and her age, Lucian LeCroix managed to conceal it. "I'd say this is certainly my lucky night then. I was hoping to meet a colleague or two at this gathering, and here you are, the first person I see. Now if I can convince you to take pity on me and show me around campus tomorrow, I will, indeed, be a fortunate man."

When Elizabeth hesitated, he rushed to add, "If you're free, of course. I realize I'm being presumptuous, but I've just driven up from Boston today, and I haven't had time to get my bearings.''

Elizabeth still wavered. She didn't much want to commit her whole Saturday to a complete stranger, and yet professional courtesy demanded that she grant him the favor. He was new in town and a colleague. And after all, did she really have anything better to do with her weekend? There was laundry, of course. And papers to grade.

And Elizabeth had to admit that Lucian LeCroix, from what she could see beneath the mask, was a very handsome man. He looked to be about thirty—ten years older than she—with black hair and dark, piercing eyes.

She could certainly do worse than be seen around campus with the charming new professor, she decided. Maybe then her students would stop calling her Sister Elizabeth behind her back, a reference not so much to her saintly qualities but to her lack of experience in earthly pleasures. How teenage girls could so quickly and accurately—and quite often viciously—size up their teachers remained a mystery to Elizabeth.

But then, so much of life was a mystery to Elizabeth.

Chapter Two

Over his shoulder, Cullen Ryan watched the rain batter the plate-glass window in the Beachway Diner as Brie Dudley topped off his coffee.

"Thanks," he mumbled absently, then turned back to the counter when she said something in response. "I'm sorry?"

She held the steaming coffee carafe in one hand as she gazed out the window behind him. She was a slim, pretty woman with curly red hair and the most amazing green eyes Cullen had ever encountered. "I was just commenting on the weather."

"Yeah," he agreed gloomily. "Not a fit night out for man nor beast, as they say."

"It's been an odd winter," Brie mused. "No snow, just rain. And now this thunderstorm. But what else would you expect on the 350th anniversary of this town's founding, right?"

Cullen shrugged. He wasn't given to superstition, and he didn't put a lot of stock in the supernatural tales that had been passed down for generations in Moriah's Landing. But he was glad anyway that he'd turned down the moonlighting gig as security guard at the Pierces' big bash tonight. He wasn't afraid of ghosts, but he'd hate like hell to be patrolling the perimeter of that huge compound, chasing away gate-crashers and sightseers and probably more than a fair share of local hoodlums looking to have a little fun and put a damper on a celebration that had excluded them.

And he should know about that type because he'd once been there. He'd been a founding member of the gang of misfits who hung out down by the wharf, decked out for trouble in their chains and chin studs and serpent tattoos. He'd once worn some of those same badges of rebellion with a fierce, misplaced pride that had almost been his downfall, but now he wore a different kind of badge. And no one was more astounded by the way he'd turned his life around than Cullen.

Funny what sleeping on the street could do for a man's perspective, he thought ironically. He'd learned a lot during his years in Boston, some of which had changed him forever and some of which he didn't much care to dwell on. It was the kind of person he was today that mattered, he tried to tell himself.

"We used to call a storm like this a widow-maker," Shamus McManus said as he turned to glance out the window. Shamus was a seasoned fish-erman who'd once worked on the same boat as Cul-len's father. Cullen had known the old geezer for years, and he knew better than to sit next to Shamus if he didn't have time for a story or two.

Besides Cullen and Shamus, the only other patron in the diner was Marley Glasglow. Dressed in a yellow rain slicker, he sat at the end of the counter, hunched over his coffee as if totally absorbed in his own thoughts. Glasglow was probably around forty, but he looked much older, a big, burly guy with a sour disposition and no visible means of support other than the few odd jobs he picked up down at the docks.

"We lost many a good man at sea on a night like this," Shamus was saying. He paused, then gave Cullen a sly glance. "A night like this can bring McFarland Leary out of his grave."

Cullen laughed. "Oh, come on now, Shamus. Don't tell me you believe in that old ghost story."

Shamus's expression turned dead serious. "I'm sixty-five years old, lad. When a man lives as long as I have, he sees things."

"You've seen Leary's ghost?" Cullen challenged.

Shamus shrugged. "I might have. They say he rises every five years. It's been that long since anyone's seen him." He glanced over his shoulder, as if expecting to see Leary's ghost peering in the window.

For the first time all evening, Glasglow looked up from his coffee, his eyes burning with an intensity that made Cullen wonder about the man's sanity. "Leary fell prey to the evil that's been the downfall of man since the beginning of time."

"And what evil is that?" Cullen asked skeptically.

"He was seduced by a woman."

Behind the counter, Brie bristled. "I hope you're not implying that all women are evil." When Glasglow refused to deny it, she said, "If women are so evil, why are most of the truly awful things in this world perpetrated by men? Why are the most vicious killers on death row almost always men? How do you explain that?"

Glasglow eyed her for a moment. "Most men kill because of a woman."

"That's ridiculous!" Brie exclaimed. She glanced at Cullen who shrugged.

"Leary was suspected of being a warlock so he was hanged on the town green," Shamus put in. "He comes back every five years because he has unfinished business in this town."

"Yeah," Glasglow muttered. "Revenge."

"Not revenge," Shamus said with a frown. "He's searching for the offspring of his unholy union with a witch. And the offspring of their offspring."

Cullen shook his head. "You've lost me, Shamus. Leary haunts this town every five years because he's looking for his great-great-great-great-grand-children?"

"Aye, and he's not the only one searching for his kin," Shamus said. "Have you never wondered why so many scientific types settle here in Moriah's Landing?"

Amused by the old man's ramblings, Cullen swiveled his stool to face him. "No, I can't say as I have. Are you suggesting it has something to do with McFarland Leary's descendants?"

"Aye, and the witch's."

"Be careful, old man," Glasglow warned. "You go sticking that nose of yours where it doesn't belong, you're apt to get it chopped off."

"Is that a threat, Marley Glasglow?" Shamus squared his shoulders, as if preparing to throw down the gauntlet. Glasglow was at least twenty years younger and thirty pounds heavier than Shamus, so Cullen decided he'd better step in before things got out of hand.

"The storm's getting worse," he commented. "Maybe we'd better all call it a night."

Brie threw him a grateful smile. "I think you're right, Cullen. I was thinking about asking my boss if we could close early."

"You're throwing us out on a night like this?" Glasglow glowered at her.

Brie shrugged. "It's only an hour till our regular closing time at ten. You'd have to leave then anyway."

"And if I refuse?"

Cullen walked over and put a hand on Glasglow's shoulder. "If you refuse, I have a nice cozy jail cell you might find to your liking."

Glasglow shoved his cup aside and stood, facing Cullen. At six feet, Cullen was tall enough, but Glasglow towered over him by a good four inches. And like Shamus, Cullen was outweighed by the man, but he knew how to deal with thugs. He'd dealt with plenty of them on the streets of Boston.

He moved slightly, so that Glasglow could glimpse the automatic he wore in a shoulder holster beneath his coat.

Glasglow eyed the gun for a moment, then his gaze met Cullen's. "You've got me shaking, boy."

Cullen's stare never wavered. "Maybe you should be."

"Considering the track record of our fine police department?" Glasglow sneered. "I'm not too worried." He walked over to the front door and drew it open. An icy gust swept through the diner, and Cullen saw Brie shiver.

Lifting the hood of his slicker over his head, Glasglow stood in the doorway for a moment, staring out into the rainy darkness.

Then he glanced over his shoulder, his gaze resting

on Brie. "The police never could find who killed
those women twenty years ago. I doubt much has
changed since then. If you ever find yourself in trouble, girl, I wouldn't be looking to the likes of him for
help."

He nodded toward Cullen, then he turned and disappeared through the doorway into the night.

"TELL ME about that castle that overlooks the sea,"
Becca said as she and Elizabeth watched the elegant
dancers swirl about the floor in the ballroom.

"You mean the Bluffs?"

"Yes, that's the one." Becca's gaze was still on
the dancers, but she looked pensive, subdued. Elizabeth wondered if something had happened during the
course of the evening to disturb her.

Except for their brief conversation in the foyer
when Elizabeth had first arrived, she'd seen little of
her friend all night. Becca had drifted away after Lucian LeCroix had come in, leaving Elizabeth alone
with the handsome professor. They'd talked for a few
minutes longer, making arrangements to meet at the
library on campus the following morning for his tour,
and then Lucian—as he insisted she call him—had
excused himself to join the party as well. Elizabeth
had been standing alone in an unobtrusive corner for
the past hour or so. She was glad that Becca had
sought her out again.

The music ended and as the couples drifted toward
the fringes of the room, Elizabeth caught a glimpse
of LeCroix. He was talking to Drew Pierce, but she
could have sworn his gaze was on her.

It was probably her imagination, she decided. A bit
of wishful thinking that a man as handsome and deb-

onair as Lucian LeCroix would look at her twice.
Since they'd spoken earlier, he hadn't approached her
again. If he was gazing in her direction now, it was
probably because of Becca.

Becca was blond and beautiful while Elizabeth was
just…Elizabeth.

Lizzie, as Cullen Ryan used to call her. Elizabeth
thought that one word, that hated nickname, spoke
volumes about the way he saw her.

"Elizabeth?" Becca touched her arm.

With an effort, Elizabeth drew her attention back
to the conversation. "Sorry. What were we talking
about? Oh, yes. The Bluffs. It was brought over from
England, stone by stone, by one of the Pierce ances-
tors, but a few years ago a man named David Bryson
acquired it. There's been bad blood between him and
the Pierces ever since. And, of course, there was
Tasha."

"Tasha?"

"Natasha Pierce." At the thought of her dead
friend, a cloak of sadness settled over Elizabeth, but
she tried to shake it off. She didn't really want to talk
about Tasha or David Bryson, but Becca was new in
town, and it was only natural she'd be curious. "Her
family never approved of David. Apart from the an-
imosity over the Bluffs, they thought he was too old
for her. She was only eighteen when they became
engaged, and David was in his thirties. She died one
night in a terrible boating accident, and her body was
never found. Since then, no one's seen David, although they say he walks the night. Supposedly, he
was horribly scarred in the explosion, and that's why
he became a recluse. That, and his guilt. The more
charitable in town think he's still grieving for Tasha.

Others say…well, never mind what others say. It's all a bit creepy, if you ask me," Elizabeth finished with a shudder.

"I think it sounds terribly romantic," Becca said softly. "I'd like to meet this David Bryson."

"No," Elizabeth said in alarm. "You don't want to do that. Don't even think it. I lost one dear friend who got mixed up with that man, and I wouldn't want to lose another."

Becca laughed. "Who said anything about getting mixed up with him? I only said I'd like to meet him."

"If you want to meet someone," Elizabeth said firmly, "there are a lot of nice guys here tonight. Take Drew Pierce, for instance. He's handsome and he's *very* rich. Most women find him totally irresistible."

"Yes, I've met Drew," Becca said in a dismissive tone. Obviously, for some reason, the town's most eligible bachelor held no particular appeal for her. But David Bryson? No, Elizabeth thought. No, no, no!

"Besides," Becca was saying, "If there are so many nice guys here tonight, why are you standing here talking to me? I haven't seen you dance once all evening."

"Oh, that's because…"

Becca lifted an elegant brow. "Yes?"

Elizabeth waved absently toward the orchestra. "I don't really care for this kind of music."

Becca gave her a speculative glance. "I realize we don't know each other all that well, but would you mind if I offered you a piece of advice?"

Elizabeth shrugged. "Of course not."

"You're a beautiful girl, Elizabeth. Very warm and caring. I've seen that side of you in the short while I've known you. But most of the time you seem so aloof. Especially around men. If you could just be a little more…approachable, you'd have them climbing all over each other to ask you to dance.''

Elizabeth glanced at her in surprise. "Who says I want to dance?"

"Every girl wants to dance," Becca said with a misty smile. She hesitated. "You know what I think? I think you use your aloofness and even your intelligence as a sanctuary. A safe place to hide away the real you so that you won't get hurt."

Elizabeth didn't know what to say to that. She couldn't deny it because there was too much truth in it.

"I've offended you, haven't I?" Becca asked worriedly.

"No, it's not that. It's just…"

"We don't know each other well enough to exchange such intimacies."

"It's not that, either," Elizabeth said. "I do feel as if I know you, and I hope we can be friends. But I've never been comfortable sharing confidences even with my closest friends."

"I can understand that. We all have things we want to keep to ourselves." A shadow moved across Becca's lovely features, making Elizabeth wonder what secrets she might harbor. "Well," she said with a bright smile that seemed a bit forced. "It's almost midnight. Maybe I should take my own advice and mingle before I turn into a pumpkin."

Elizabeth didn't think that would happen. She knew very little of Becca's life before she came to Moriah's Landing, but it was obvious the woman knew how to handle herself in social situations. Elizabeth watched with no small amount of envy as her new friend drifted through the crowd with the utmost confidence. She seemed perfectly comfortable in her surroundings even though she knew hardly anyone at the ball.

Elizabeth, on the other hand, had grown up in Moriah's Landing and while her parents weren't as wealthy as the Pierces, her life had been one of privilege. She should be the one at ease in such a setting, but she wasn't. She longed to be home, snuggled in bed with one of her favorite books, the way she spent most of her evenings. If she wasn't careful, she could easily become a recluse.

Like David Bryson.

THE CLOCK in the foyer struck midnight just as Elizabeth slipped out of the ballroom. She'd meant to seek refuge inside the library across the hall, but instead, she made her way to the rear of the house where a glass-domed solarium would give her a breathtaking view of the storm.

She opened the door and stepped inside. The room was dark and fragrant with exotic blossoms, and very cold. Elizabeth didn't turn on the light, but used the occasional flashes of lightning to make her way toward the back of the solarium, where long rows of French doors opened onto a flagstone patio and garden.

She rubbed her hands up and down her bare arms, wishing for her velvet cloak. Surely such a chill couldn't be good for the tropical varieties of plants and ferns which grew jungle-thick beneath the glass dome.

As she neared the back of the solarium, Elizabeth realized why the temperature had plunged inside the room. One of the French doors had blown wide, and gusts of icy wind and rain whipped through the opening.

She rushed over to fasten the door, but it resisted her tug. As she struggled with the latch, something moved outside beyond the patio. A flash of color, nothing more. A brief flare of yellow that melted into blackness.

Then the wind slammed the door to with such force that Elizabeth had to jump back to keep her hand from being smashed. She slipped on the wet floor and lost her balance, crashing backward into a plant table. Expensive glazed pots shattered against flagstones.

She struggled to sit up, but the hoops beneath her voluminous skirts kept her off balance.

"Damn," she muttered, wincing as a shard from one of the shattered pots bit into her palm. She lifted her hand to see if the cut was bleeding, but for some reason, her gaze was drawn skyward. Among the trailing leaves of some lush vine, something swayed from the rafters.

Elizabeth propped herself on her elbows, staring upward. What was that—

In a flare of lightning, she saw a pale face staring down at her.

A ghost! her terrified mind first thought, and her heart began to hammer painfully against her rib cage.

But then, an instant later, she saw the rope.

Chapter Three

"Who found the body?"

The curt question broke into Elizabeth's chaotic thoughts as she stood outside the solarium with the Pierces. She looked up, expecting to see one of the uniformed officers who'd arrived on the scene a few minutes after William Pierce had called the police, or perhaps even the police chief himself. Instead, her gaze collided with Cullen Ryan's.

And her heart almost stopped.

She hadn't seen him this close since he'd moved back to Moriah's Landing several months ago. Elizabeth thought she'd conquered her old feelings for him once and for all, but then he'd gone and done the unexpected. The unthinkable. He'd gone and made himself respectable.

And now she was all confused again. She stared up at him helplessly.

His short, dark hair glistened with raindrops, and his eyes—gray, like a winter sky—were cool and assessing. He wasn't overly tall, probably around six feet, but he carried himself in that edgy, confident manner which had always made him seem taller. He was dressed darkly in a heavy long coat over a black

V-neck sweater and black jeans, and Elizabeth couldn't take her eyes off him. He was so good-looking!

And a young woman was so dead.

Elizabeth would do well to remember why Cullen was there. She tried to convince herself that her reaction to him was due to her lingering shock, not just in finding the body but in discovering the victim's identity. And it *had* been a shock.

Once she'd turned on the light in the solarium, she'd recognized almost at once the pale face, the dark, flowing hair. The delicate features that remained winsome even in death.

And with recognition had come the shakes. Elizabeth had started to tremble violently, and she hadn't been able to stop. Someone had fetched her velvet cloak earlier, and she clutched it now like a lifeline. She opened her mouth to answer Cullen, but her teeth were chattering so badly she couldn't speak.

William came to her rescue. "Elizabeth found the poor girl. It's been quite traumatic for all of us, as you can imagine."

When Elizabeth had first informed William and Drew of her grisly discovery, they'd tried to leave the ballroom discreetly, so as not to alarm or panic their guests. Luckily, Mayor Thane had already departed the ball. Otherwise he would have undoubtedly insinuated himself into the situation in such a way as to garner as much press for himself as possible—and conversely, as much unfavourable publicity for his potential rival as he could generate. Bad enough that Zachary, Drew's younger brother, noting the grim expression on his father's face, had followed them to the solarium and a few minutes later, Geoffrey Pierce,

William's brother, had shown up as well. Now that the police were on the scene, word would spread soon enough among the guests, if it hadn't already.

William stepped forward now and offered his hand to Cullen. "I'm William Pierce, by the way."

"Yes, I know who you are," Cullen said without expression as he shook hands with the man. "I'm Detective Ryan."

William glanced over Cullen's shoulder. "Where's Chief Redfern? Shouldn't he be here?"

"He's out of town, but he's been notified. The roads in and out of Moriah's Landing are a mess from the storm. It may be hours before he can make it through."

William frowned. "Shouldn't we wait for him?"

"I'm afraid we can't wait. Deterioration of the body could break down any DNA evidence that might be present. We'll need to collect samples as soon as Dr. Vogel arrives," Cullen said, referring to the medical examiner.

"What about the state police?"

"This is our jurisdiction."

"I see." William still didn't look convinced. "That all sounds well and good, young man, but you haven't been with the police department all that long, have you? Are you sure you have the experience for this sort of investigation?"

Annoyance flitted across Cullen's brow. "I appreciate your concern, Mr. Pierce, but I assure you I'm a trained investigator."

"Yes, well, I'm sorry to be so blunt, but you seem a little young to me to be a detective."

He was twenty-four, Elizabeth thought, and age was relative. She knew that better than anyone.

If Cullen had remained with the Boston Police Department, chances were he probably wouldn't have made detective for another few years. But in Moriah's Landing, any big-city police-force experience automatically propelled an officer to the head of the pack. Most of the other law-enforcement personnel, Chief Redfern included, had only spotty experience and the minimum amount of training required by the Commonwealth. Whether William Pierce realized it or not, the town was lucky to have Cullen.

"I know what I'm doing," he said coolly.

"I hope you do." There was an indefinable edge in William's voice. Was his concern really due to Cullen's age, or because of Cullen's background? Before he'd left town, Cullen had had more than one brush with the local authorities. The charges were never anything too serious—vandalism, joy-riding, crimes of that nature, and because they could never be proven, the complaints were invariably dropped. But people had never had any doubt about Cullen's guilt, and they always suspected those petty misdemeanors were a prelude to something more serious, something potentially more deadly.

Did William Pierce harbor doubts about Cullen's transformation as so many others in town did?

Elizabeth didn't. Not really. She'd always known there was a good side to Cullen. He'd just never allowed anyone to see it.

What was it Becca had said to her earlier? *You use your aloofness and even your intelligence as a sanctuary, a safe place to hide away the real you so you won't get hurt.*

Had Cullen's juvenile delinquency been his sanctuary? Elizabeth wondered.

He was staring down at her, watching her closely, and her breath caught painfully in her throat. Would she never get over this silly crush? This terrible yearning that caused every nerve ending in her stomach to quiver if he so much as glanced at her?

"You're the one who found the body?" he asked her.

She nodded, buying herself a moment to collect her poise. "Yes, in the solarium. Her name is Bethany Peters."

One dark brow lifted. "You knew her?"

"She was a student at Heathrow College. She was in my Theories of Criminal Behavior class last semester." Elizabeth tried not to dwell on the irony.

"Was she a guest at the party?" He addressed this question to William Pierce.

"No, none of us had ever seen her before."

Cullen turned back to Elizabeth. "What were you doing in the solarium?"

She hesitated. "The ballroom was very crowded. I just wanted a chance to catch my breath." Would he think she'd been dancing all night instead of people-watching from a secluded corner? Instead of daydreaming about him?

One could only hope.

"Why the solarium?"

"It has this wonderful glass dome. I wanted to watch the storm a bit." The intensity of his gaze made Elizabeth even more nervous. Her hand crept to her throat, and she found herself explaining, "It's an air mass thunderstorm rather than an organized system, you see, and I wanted to observe the redevelopment of new convection along the outflow of the previous cells." *Shut up, shut up, shut up,* she admonished herself, but she couldn't seem to stop babbling. "The main cell, of course, was well into its dissipating stage by that time," she finished lamely.

Cullen ran a hand through his short, spiky hair. "Uh, right. Do you have an idea what time you left the ballroom?"

"Midnight. I heard the clock in the foyer chime." Elizabeth pressed her lips together to keep from blurting out any more irrelevant facts. She had the unfortunate habit of resorting to trivia when she got nervous, and she had always been nervous around Cullen.

"Did you see anyone else in the foyer? In the hallway outside the solarium? Anyone lurking outside?"

"No. Maybe. I'm not sure." She drew an unsteady breath and told him about the open door in the solarium and the yellow flash she'd seen beyond the terrace. "It might have been nothing more than a reflection. I can't be sure. I certainly can't say beyond a shadow of a doubt that it was a person."

"If it was, we're not going to find any footprints in this weather," he said grimly.

Elizabeth's fingers tightened around the fastener on her cloak. "I don't think it very likely, but I suppose it's possible someone could have been inside the room when I first entered, and then left through that door. I didn't turn on a light."

"Why not?"

"As I said, I slipped away from the party to be alone for a few minutes. I didn't want anyone to see me."

Cullen's glance sharpened. "Were you afraid someone would follow you into the solarium?"

As if. "No. I just thought someone might see the

light and become curious. And, also, it was easier to observe the storm in the darkness.''

"I see. When you went back to close the door, that's when you saw the body?"

She nodded. "I lost my balance on the wet floor and fell. For some reason, I looked up and I saw her hanging from one of the steel supports...." Elizabeth broke off, shuddering in spite of herself.

She wasn't unfamiliar with death. In her Criminal Investigations courses at Heathrow, she taught her students how to dissect crime scenes analytically and view murder victims objectively. As a graduate student, she'd interned with the Worcester Police Department in order to research her doctoral thesis, and just a few months ago, she'd attended a series of seminars conducted by an FBI profiler. She knew crime. She lived and breathed crime.

But when the victim was someone you knew... someone so young...

"I'll need statements from all of you," Cullen said to the Pierces who stood clustered behind Elizabeth. "For now, I want everyone to remain out here. We need to keep the crime scene as virgin as possible."

Elizabeth winced. "I'm afraid...that is, the solarium may already have been compromised."

"Someone besides you has been in there?" Cullen asked sharply.

"We rushed in without thinking when Elizabeth told us what she'd found," Drew explained. "She tried to keep us out, but we couldn't know for certain the girl was dead. We thought we might be able to help her."

Cullen glanced at Elizabeth. "How many went inside?"

"All of them," she admitted gloomily.

He shook his head in frustration. "We'll have to cross-check fingerprints then. I'll also need a copy of the guest list." He turned to the uniformed officer who stood directly behind him. "Make sure guards remain at all the exits. No one leaves, no one gets in without my say-so. I don't care who it is," he said pointedly at the Pierces. "I don't care what excuses they give you."

"Surely you don't expect everyone to wait around here indefinitely," Geoffrey Pierce, Drew's uncle, complained. "I have things to do."

"At this hour?" Cullen gave him a speculative look. "What kind of things would they be?"

Geoffrey didn't answer, just stood there looking unpleasant. A tall, slender man with thinning blond hair, he hadn't managed the approach to middle age with quite the same grace as his older brother, William. And he didn't seem to have William's compassion. He was handsome, as all the Pierces were, but something about his expression, about the cruel set of his lips, made him seem at once sinister and weak.

Drew put a hand on the man's arm. "Detective Ryan is right, Uncle Geoffrey. We screwed up. Let's not make things worse." To Cullen he said, "We'll do everything we can to cooperate."

"I'm counting on that." Cullen took a pair of latex gloves from his overcoat pocket and snapped them on. He handed another pair to Elizabeth. "Show me the body, Elizabeth."

THE FIRST THING Cullen noticed about the solarium was the temperature. The room was still frigid even though Elizabeth said she'd closed the outside door.

He could feel the chill though his overcoat, but then, the heavy fabric was still damp from the rain.

He wondered now, as he followed Elizabeth toward the back of the solarium, if he might have been able to prevent the tragedy if he'd accepted the moonlighting job as a security guard for the Pierces. Probably not. So far, it appeared that the murderer had been able to slip in and out without being detected by any of the other guards or guests which suggested to Cullen that the suspect was someone familiar with the Pierce compound. Someone who had either come in the front gate as a guest, or through the back entrance with the hired help.

But that hardly narrowed the field. Party-goers had come from all over the state, and in Moriah's Landing alone, half the population had either received invitations to the party or been hired to work in some capacity at the compound.

In short, the killer could be anyone, Cullen thought grimly as he tugged at the neckline of his sweater.

The solarium was crowded with plants. Some of the tree ferns grew all the way to the top of the dome while a maze of sinewy vines coiled around the rafters and crept downward, inching away from the sunlight. Hanging baskets trailed lacy fronds that brushed against Cullen's shoulders, making him think of spiders. He found the atmosphere inside the solarium suffocating, as if the plants were sucking all the air from the room.

Elizabeth had stopped in front of him and was staring at him curiously. "Are you all right?"

"I'm fine." His tone was more clipped than he'd meant it to be.

She cocked her head, still regarding him. "It's

rather close in here, with all the plants. You're not claustrophobic, are you?''

He glanced at her warily. "Claustrophobic?''

"An abnormal dread of being in closed or narrow spaces.''

"I know what it means,'' Cullen said dryly. "But only you would put it that way.''

"What way?''

"Only you would use the exact dictionary definition. Word for word, I'll bet.''

She lifted her chin. "What's wrong with being precise?''

"Nothing.'' She wouldn't understand even if he explained it to her. People with a high IQ seemed to live in their own little world. "I don't have claustrophobia,'' he said with an impatient shrug. "I just don't care for all these damn plants.''

"Well, maybe you have botanophobia. Fear of plants.''

"What I *don't* have is time,'' he snapped. "Let's get on with this.''

"Of course.'' She gave him a cool glance as she turned and walked to the back of the solarium without another word.

Cullen hoped he hadn't hurt her feelings, but, damn, she could be so annoying. There seemed to be no end to the trivia she'd stuffed inside that head of hers. She'd always been way too smart—and far too superior—for her own good in Cullen's opinion. That was one of the reasons she'd had so much trouble in school. Bad enough she was such an Einstein, but did she have to rub people's noses in it?

It was a shame, too, because she wasn't a bad-looking girl. Cullen supposed that some might even consider her attractive, in a sisterly sort of way. Nice hair. Nice eyes. Slight build.

She'd matured since he'd left town six years ago, but she was still very young. He had a hard time thinking of her as anything other than the bratty little kid he'd tried to protect from the bullies who'd ragged on her in school. Although, to this day, he couldn't figure out why he'd bothered. She'd made it clear from the first she didn't want or need help from the likes of him.

Fair enough, he supposed. She wasn't only brilliant, she was rich to boot. She came from the ritzy part of town, and Cullen had grown up down by the docks. Her parents were scientists; his old man had been a drunk. They didn't exactly travel in the same social circles, he and Elizabeth.

She'd stopped in front of him again, her head tilted skyward. Cullen glanced up. The body dangled about ten feet from the floor from a steel girder that helped support the glass dome.

Cullen's blood went cold with shock even though he'd had plenty of time to prepare himself. It didn't matter how prepped he was or how many times he worked a crime scene, murder always got him in the gut.

Especially when the victim was very young.

She couldn't have been more than eighteen or nineteen. Someone's daughter. Someone's sister. Snuffed out by a cold-blooded murderer who'd left her hanging there like a piece of meat in a butcher-shop freezer.

"It's not a suicide," Elizabeth murmured.

No, it wasn't a suicide, he thought grimly.

"I can't see any wounds," she added, "But I'm

certain she was dead before she was hanged. Otherwise, there would be…visible signs.''

A protruding tongue, for one thing. ''How the hell did he get her up there?'' Cullen muttered.

Out of the corner of his eye, he saw Elizabeth shiver. She'd been the girl's professor at Heathrow, but he was willing to bet there wasn't more than a year or two difference in their ages. In spite of himself, he felt his protective instinct stirring again. She shouldn't be here. He shouldn't have let her come back in here.

''This won't take long,'' he said. ''I just need to ask you a few questions about finding the body. I want you to show me where everyone was standing when the Pierces came in here. Tell me about their reactions, what was said, anything like that you can remember. Then you can wait outside with everyone else.''

She turned to stare up at him, her expression earnest. ''I'd really like to stay until Dr. Vogel examines the body.''

Cullen shook his head. ''That's out of the question.''

''Why?''

''Do I have to state the obvious? You found the body.''

''But what does—'' She stopped abruptly, her eyes going wide. ''Are you saying I'm a suspect?''

He shrugged. ''Everyone here is a suspect. I'm not ruling anyone out at this point.''

''But—'' She broke off again. ''Of course. I understand. You have to take that approach. But I really think I can help you. I know about crime-scene investigation. I'm a professional, just like you.''

"Not exactly like me. You aren't wearing a badge," he said bluntly. "If you really want to help, just answer my questions. That's all I need from you."

She looked as if she wanted to protest, but decided against it. Pursing her lips, she turned her back on him.

He'd probably hurt her feelings again, but it couldn't be helped. Ph.D. or not, Cullen wasn't about to involve a civilian in his investigation. For one thing, bringing in an outside consultant was a tricky business. Egos could get in the way, and secondly, he had his reservations about Elizabeth's competence.

Oh, she was plenty intelligent. No question about that. But it had been Cullen's experience that no amount of classroom theory or book knowledge in the world could take the place of plain old-fashioned street smarts, the kind learned the hard way. And for all her education and degrees, Cullen doubted she'd ever really been put to the test. After she answered his questions, he'd send her packing.

"There's a ladder against one of the walls," she said.

He frowned. "What?"

"You asked how he'd gotten her up there. I saw a ladder in here earlier. Mr. Pierce said it's used to cut away dead leaves from the vines and the larger plants, and to change the bulbs when the ultraviolet lights burn out."

"Did anyone touch it that you saw?"

"No. Mr. Pierce suggested his sons use it to cut her down, but I discouraged that. I warned them we had to leave her as we'd found her."

At least she'd done that right, he thought grudgingly. "We'll dust the ladder for prints," he said, ignoring the expectant look on Elizabeth's face.

He studied the immediate area underneath the body. The floor was a mess with broken pottery scattered about and muddy water all over the flagstones near the French doors. Cullen could see at least one partial footprint in the sludge.

He motioned to the floor. "Was all this here when you came in?"

Elizabeth bit her lip. "The floor was wet, but I knocked over the pots when I fell."

He'd been afraid of that. "Is that your footprint?"

"Yes, I think so."

"We'll have to check it out anyway. We may need your shoes for verification."

"Of course."

They both fell silent for a moment, then Elizabeth said softly, "You noticed, didn't you?"

"Noticed what?"

"There's no blood on the body or on the floor. And look at the color of her skin. She looks as if she's been exposed to extreme temperature, but there's no frostbite."

Cullen had seen the same thing, but he'd kept his observation to himself. He'd learned a long time ago to make no assumptions.

"My guess is she was killed somewhere else and brought here," Elizabeth said. "She could have been dead for several days. The killer probably kept her in a cooler or freezer somewhere until the time was right."

"Meaning?" Cullen glanced at her curiously. Whether he wanted to admit it or not, something about the confident manner in which she spoke had his attention.

"Until he was ready for someone to find her." Elizabeth's gaze moved upward, where the body of Bethany Peters stirred gently in a slight draft from a heating vent. "He put her on display. She was left here, like this, for a reason. The killer is trying to tell us something."

Cullen knew instantly what she meant. One-time crime-of-passion killers would only take the time to move the body of their victim in order to dump it in a remote location or to try and throw off the police. They wouldn't flaunt it. Neither would a professional hit man. There was only one type of killer who would.

Elizabeth turned to Cullen, her eyes deeply troubled. "This is a very bad thing, Cullen."

His gaze lifted to the body. It didn't take a genius to figure that out.

THE MOMENT the medical examiner arrived, Elizabeth was expelled from the solarium.

"We'll take it from here," Cullen told her firmly.

"But I'd like to help—"

"If we need your help, we'll ask for it." He must have realized how harsh his words sounded because he almost at once altered his tone. "I appreciate everything you've done so far, but this is a police investigation. You need to wait outside with everyone else."

When she still resisted, his grasp tightened on her elbow. "Come on, Elizabeth. Cut me a break here."

"But you can't seriously consider me a suspect," she protested. "If you'd listen to your brain for a moment instead of your ego, you'd realize I could help you.'' She winced. That hadn't come out at all right. She hadn't meant to goad him, but somehow, around Cullen, she always managed to say the wrong thing.

''You've done quite enough already,'' he said coolly.

''If you're referring to letting the Pierces come into the solarium, I had no authority to keep them out,'' she defended. ''I'm not a police officer.''

He arched a brow. ''Precisely my point.''

''Just let me stay while Dr. Vogel examines the body. I want to hear what he says about cause of death.''

''Out.''

''Cullen—''

''*Out.*''

He opened the solarium door and gave her an un-ceremonious little push into the hallway. The door closed firmly behind her.

The Pierces were still in the hallway, and they gazed at her curiously.

''I take it your services are no longer required,'' Drew commented.

''Cops can be so…infuriating.'' The latex gloves snapped loudly as Elizabeth peeled them off.

''They do tend to have a one-track mind,'' William sympathized. ''But in this case, I have to agree with Detective Ryan. A murder scene is no place for a young lady.''

''But I teach criminology,'' she protested. ''I'm not unfamiliar with crime scenes.''

''You can't be more than a day over twenty years old. Hardly more than a child. If Natasha were still alive, I certainly wouldn't want her subjected to such

a gruesome scene.'' Pain flashed in William's blue
eyes, and whatever annoyance Elizabeth had been
harboring toward him for his comments about her age
vanished. Tasha's death had affected them all, but especially her family. It was obvious that her father still
grieved her passing. That was why he hadn't been
able to forgive David Bryson and probably never
would.

But had Bryson been able to forgive himself? Elizabeth wondered. Or had his guilt driven him to do
unspeakable evil, as some of the townspeople suspected?

Careful, she warned herself. *Don't let your imagination get the better of you.*

They had absolutely no evidence thus far linking
David Bryson to Bethany's murder. Nothing except
an innate distrust of the man, and Elizabeth knew she
was prejudiced in that regard. Tasha had been her
friend.

If she wasn't careful, such a biased perspective
would end up proving Cullen's point—that she had
no place in a murder investigation.

''They won't find anything,'' Geoffrey Pierce murmured in a strange, offhand manner, his gaze on the
solarium door. ''That girl was dead before she was
hanged.''

Elizabeth had come to the same conclusion, but it
wasn't exactly admiration she felt for Geoffrey's keen
perception.

Earlier, when they'd all rushed into the solarium,
the other Pierces had been deeply disturbed by the
sight of the body, especially Zachary, who'd turned a
bit green when his father suggested that he and Drew
find a way to cut her down. The same look of horror

and compassion had emanated from all the Pierces' blue eyes—all except for Geoffrey's.

In his eyes only a cool curiosity had gleamed.

Elizabeth had to wonder about a man, a nonprofessional, who could remain so stoic and unaffected in the face of such horror.

Her gaze on him narrowed. "Why do you think Cullen won't find any evidence?"

He shrugged. "Because whoever did that knew what he was doing."

"He?"

"Given your field of expertise, I'm sure you know as well as I do that crimes of this nature are almost always masterminded by white males. Serial killers seem to be a unique affliction to our race and gender." He didn't seem especially disturbed by his conclusion.

"Serial killer?" Elizabeth said, feigning surprise. "Who said anything about a serial killer?"

Geoffrey gave her an enigmatic smile. "Don't tell me the same thought didn't cross your mind when you saw her hanging there. The way the body was put on exhibition? What else could it be?"

"An act of rage," Elizabeth said. "A crime of passion."

He shook his head. "You don't believe that. You know what we're dealing with here as well as I do."

Elizabeth had studied crimes such as this in both her undergraduate and graduate courses. She'd learned a long time ago what it meant when a murderer "signed" his kill.

But she couldn't help wondering how Geoffrey Pierce knew.

And would another body soon follow that would prove his point?

Chapter Four

The storm had moved out to sea an hour or so earlier, but Elizabeth could still see flashes of lightning in the distance as she sat in her parked car down the street from Krauter's Funeral Home. The downpour had finally abated into an icy drizzle that glistened on the cobblestone pavement like a scene from a French Impressionist painting.

The hour was very late, after three in the morning, and for a moment, Elizabeth was struck by the eerie silence, the preternatural peace that had settled over the night in the wake of bone-chilling violence.

Cloistered in the leathery confines of her new car, she could almost believe that the last few hours had never happened. But they had. A young woman was dead. A student had been murdered, and Elizabeth had discovered the body. No seminar or classroom or degree in the world could have prepared her for that grisly sight.

She watched nervously as the gleaming black hearse carrying Bethany Peters's body slowly glided past her. The windows were so darkly tinted in the vehicle that she couldn't make out any of the occupants, but she knew that besides the driver there was one other attendant. She'd been present at the Pierce mansion when the mortuary people had arrived to pick up the corpse.

Tomorrow, Bethany would be transported to a nearby hospital where an autopsy would be performed, and the cause of death would likely be determined. But for tonight she would remain in a cooler at Krauter's.

A squad car—flashers blacked out, siren silenced—followed the hearse, and Elizabeth ducked down in her seat even though she was fairly certain Cullen had remained at the mansion. He had hours of interviews to conduct and acres of grounds to search, but he would abandon everything in a heartbeat if he had even an inkling of what Elizabeth was up to.

She tamped down a momentary reservation. Okay, so what she had in mind wasn't exactly brilliant. Probably wasn't even a good idea. She would be interfering with an official police investigation. She could be fined, even do some serious jail time if she were caught, but Elizabeth didn't see that she had any other choice. When she'd approached Cullen again later about examining the body, he'd told her no way. No way in hell, to be exact.

"Just give me one minute, Cullen. That's all I'm asking for. I need to see the body again. I think I saw something—"

"Saw what?"

"I'm...not sure."

He ran his fingers through his dark hair, a gesture that was both familiar and endearing—or would have been, if Elizabeth hadn't been so thoroughly irritated with him.

The feeling, evidently, was mutual. "I don't have time for this, Elizabeth."

"Why do you have to be so stubborn? Can't you just admit you may need my help?"

"With what?"

"The *investigation*, for crying out loud."

He gazed down at her for a long, tense moment, his gray eyes cool, remote. Sexy. "Haven't you ever heard that old saying, Elizabeth? Those who can, do; those who can't, teach."

That hurt.

She gave him a disparaging look. "Are you afraid to let me see the body, Cullen?"

"Why would I be afraid?"

"Maybe you think I'll find something you didn't."

His expression became rigid then, and Elizabeth had known she'd gone too far. Again. She'd pressed him way past irritation all the way to anger. Maybe even nudged him into contempt.

"Just stay out of my way, okay? And don't let me catch you playing Nancy Drew with this case. I'm warning you, Elizabeth…"

Nancy Drew! The nerve, Elizabeth fumed, as she huddled more deeply into her leather seat. Did Nancy Drew have a Ph.D. in criminology? Had Nancy Drew struck up an e-mail correspondence with one of the most famous profilers in the Behavioral Science Unit at Quantico? Did Nancy Drew have an IQ of—

Okay, okay, a little voice complained inside her. *Enough already. You're starting to annoy me, for God's sake.*

It was true she never knew when to give up, but Elizabeth had always considered persistence a virtue, not a vice. And she was certain she could help solve this case if Cullen would just give her a chance.

But he was hung up on her age, just like everyone else. If she were a man, if it had taken her the usual amount of time to complete her graduate degree and subsequent field training, no one would question her expertise. No one would think twice about using her on this case.

But she was only twenty, looked even younger, and because of that, Cullen was shutting her out.

Be honest, that same little voice taunted her. *Are you really upset because he won't use you in the investigation, or because he still sees you as an immature schoolgirl? Someone he could never be interested in romantically or...sexually.*

Elizabeth sighed. She might as well be a brain without a body for all the male attention she elicited. Unless you counted Dr. Paul Fortier, a biology professor at Heathrow, and since his reputation with the opposite sex was a bit notorious, Elizabeth didn't think she could consider him a conquest.

Besides, she wasn't absolutely certain he'd made a pass at her. She'd had a high fever when he'd approached her a few weeks ago after a faculty meeting. It was entirely possible she'd misinterpreted his gesture—and what he'd said to her—but whatever the case, there was something about the man that creeped her out big-time. The way his eyes had seemed to slide all over her when he'd looked at her. The way her skin had crawled when he'd touched her.

Shivering, she rose in her seat and glanced out the window. Tires swished against the wet pavement as the hearse and the police car turned into the drive of the narrow, three-story structure which housed not only the mortuary and crematorium, but the private residence of Ned Krauter, the town mortician.

Out of respect for the dead, or perhaps the late hour, car doors closed quietly as the attendants got out of the hearse and the officer climbed out of the squad car. The three men stood talking for a moment, and Elizabeth let her gaze scan the funeral home.

Windows were lit on the second story of the building where Mr. Krauter resided, and on the ground floor where the mortuary facilities were located.

The third story had been converted into an apartment for lease, and in spite of all the activity below, the windows up there remained dark. Exactly what kind of person would want to live over a funeral home and crematorium, Elizabeth couldn't imagine, but her concern tonight wasn't for Mr. Krauter's lodger, but with Mr. Krauter himself, and how she might be able to sneak into the building without him knowing.

It was a risky proposition, but Elizabeth desperately wanted a closer look at Bethany's body. Once the postmortem took place, it might be too late. Whatever it was that had disturbed her earlier might be lost forever.

After another moment of quiet conversation, the attendants opened the back doors of the hearse and slid out the gurney. A sheet covering the body fluttered in the wind as the attendants wheeled the gurney to the back door of the mortuary. Once they and the police officer had disappeared inside, Elizabeth got out of her car and ran along the street toward the funeral home, clutching her cloak tightly against her. Now that the storm had passed, the temperature was plummeting, and she could feel the chill seeping into her bones.

As she'd expected, the back entrance had been left temporarily unlocked. Elizabeth opened the door a crack and peered inside. No one was about, so she slipped in.

She'd never been in that portion of the funeral home, but the layout of the house was not unlike that of dozens of other clapboard homes in Moriah's Landing.

In fact, the entire structure had once been a private residence. Ned Krauter's grandfather had immigrated from Europe right after the First World War, bringing with him the family mortuary trade which had been passed down for generations. Why he'd left Europe no one seemed to know, but soon after his arrival in Moriah's Landing, he'd bought the large house for a song from a widow who'd found herself in a desperate financial situation after her third husband had unexpectedly committed suicide.

Krauter had turned the residence into a funeral home, and when he'd died back in the fifties, he'd left his only son a flourishing business which Krauter the Second had, in turn, passed on to his only son, along with an assortment of odd family traits that had been for years the source of no small amount of speculation in Moriah's Landing.

The current Mr. Krauter had never married and thus had no heir. Elizabeth couldn't decide whether she considered his childless state a pity or a blessing.

The room she stood in had once been the kitchen of the original residence. The sinks and cupboards had been upgraded to stainless steel, but most everything else had been stripped away. It was now used as a receiving room—the entry point for bodies to the funeral home. There were signs posted in prominent

areas which proclaimed that the room met all state
and federal requirements for blood-borne pathogens.
Although it wasn't a formaldehyde area, Elizabeth
could smell a strong disinfectant that made her
slightly queasy.

Several doors radiated from the receiving room,
most of them clearly marked. The embalming room,
straight ahead. To the right, near where she stood, the
crematory. To her left, the coolers. To her far right,
an unmarked door that led presumably into the other
areas of the funeral home.

It would take only a few moments for the attendants and the officer to transfer the body to one of
the coolers, and then they'd come back in here. The
officer would probably remain on guard all night, in
his squad car she hoped. If he stayed near the coolers
or in the receiving area, Elizabeth would have a big
problem. But she didn't think that too likely. People
in Moriah's Landing were nothing if not superstitious,
and that included most of the police force.

All she needed to do was find a place to hide until
the coast was clear. She surveyed her options once
again. The embalming room. The crematory. The unmarked door.

Duh, as her students would say.

Elizabeth opened door number three and cautiously
stepped through.

A narrow, dark hallway stretched before her, and
she hesitated just inside the door, trying to get her
bearings. But it was no use. The corridor was win-
dowless, making navigation highly precarious. Elizabeth hated to use her flashlight, but unless she
wanted to stumble around and risk detection, she had

no other choice. Pressing the switch, she angled the beam down the hallway.

If she could locate the lobby or the chapel, that wouldn't be so bad. She could find a pew and sit quietly. Meditate on how much trouble she would be in if Cullen were to find her there.

Maybe he would even threaten her with...dire repercussions. For a moment Elizabeth let herself fantasize about the possibilities.

Then she snapped out of it. Kinky wishful thinking, coming from a girl—a woman—who'd barely even been kissed.

She suppressed a sigh just as a light came on at the end of the hallway and she heard footsteps. Someone was coming down the stairs.

Elizabeth's heart started to pump in overdrive. There was a door just ahead, and she rushed toward it, the skirts of her costume rustling noisily. She doused her flashlight and melted inside the room just as the footsteps sounded down the hallway.

They came closer. Closer. And then they slowed.

Elizabeth held her breath. She glanced around frantically for a place to hide, but she could see nothing in the darkened room, and she didn't dare turn her flashlight back on.

The door opened, and she pressed herself against the wall behind it, praying that the abundant folds of her dress would not spill out and reveal her hiding place.

For a moment, her luck seemed to hold. Nothing happened. Nothing moved. Elizabeth didn't even dare breathe. She stood there, pulse hammering in her throat as she tried to will away whoever stood on the other side of the door.

And then the light came on, and she blinked, certain that she'd been caught. When her eyes became accustomed to the blinding glare, she glanced around.

Whoever stood in the doorway did not come into the room, but Elizabeth wasn't alone.

Not five feet from where she stood squeezed against the wall, a woman she didn't recognize rested peacefully in a satin-lined coffin.

"Good night, Mrs. Presco," a voice whispered from the doorway.

THIRTY MINUTES LATER, Elizabeth crept from the funeral home lobby where she'd been hiding and glanced down the hallway. The light at the end of the corridor had been extinguished once again when Mr. Krauter had gone back upstairs, and as far as Elizabeth could tell, the coast was clear.

Earlier, she'd waited in the viewing room with Mrs. Presco just long enough for the door to close and for Mr. Krauter—presumably the visitor—to disappear down the hallway toward the receiving area where he'd undoubtedly gone to oversee the arrival of Bethany's remains.

While Elizabeth had been scrunched behind the door in the viewing room, she'd tried to tell herself there was nothing wrong with Mr. Krauter conversing with the dead. It was rather…sweet.

But images had started to form in her head, visions that had made her break out in a cold sweat. She'd barely allowed Mr. Krauter time to get to the receiving area before she'd opened the door of the viewing room and all but tumbled into the hallway. Then she'd found herself a new place to hide until she'd heard him return to his living quarters upstairs.

Satisfied that he wasn't coming back downstairs, that the two attendants had gone home and the police officer was standing guard somewhere outside, Elizabeth decided it was time to make her move.

She paused in the corridor now, listening to the quiet of the funeral home. Like any old structure, the house had its fair share of creaks and rattles. Cold drafts. Nothing that was overly alarming.

But she was still uneasy, and she pulled her cloak tightly around her as she tiptoed toward the receiving area. A light over the sink had been left on, and she could see at once the room was empty. She was tempted to draw open the back door and try to determine where the police officer might be. But if he was just outside, he would see her. Best to proceed on the assumption that he was safely ensconced in his squad car. Maybe even snoozing by this time.

Before she had a chance to lose her nerve—or regain her sensibilities—Elizabeth hurried over to the cooler-room door, pulled it open, and stepped inside. The door closed behind her with a swish, and she resisted the urge to try the knob to make sure she wasn't locked inside. If she was trapped, it might be better to prolong her ignorance.

The room was completely dark. Elizabeth groped along the wall for the light switch, but when she couldn't find it, she realized the control was probably on the other side of the wall, in the receiving area. The funeral-home personnel would know to turn on the lights before entering the vault-like cooler room.

She flicked on her flashlight. The room came slowly into focus as the beam played off stainless-steel fixtures and a torturous-looking device suspended from the ceiling that she presumed was used for lifting and lowering bodies. She remembered reading once that back injuries were prevalent in the mortuary business.

Spotting the metal cooler, she moved toward it, gooseflesh prickling at the back of her neck.

Being alone in a mortuary cooler room was not for the faint of heart. Elizabeth wasn't usually squeamish, but she had a healthy respect for the unknown. The metaphysical. The dark forces at work in the world which couldn't be explained by any amount of scientific research and experimentation.

Early on in her studies, she'd become interested in more than just means, motive and opportunity in murder. Criminal personality profilers had long since determined that most serial killers shared certain characteristics from their childhood. The big three warning signs, as they were known, were: chronic bedwetting, the torture of small animals and an obsession with pyrotechnics. In addition, most had suffered child abuse. But Elizabeth had wanted to know if there were other forces at play. She'd wanted to delve even more deeply into the killer's mind to determine if there was a kind of base instinct that drove men to kill, not just once but over and over.

In graduate school, her fascination had taken a new twist. Could there be something more than instinct or abuse that drove a mind to the dark side? What about where the killer grew up, where he lived, where he worked?

In other words, could a *place* be evil?

Elizabeth didn't know why, but ever since childhood, she'd been very attuned to the strange vibrations in Moriah's Landing. Sometimes when she lay awake at night, she could sense the supernatural undercurrents that rippled through the town. She could feel the evil that lingered from the witch executions of the 1600s and from the murders of twenty years ago. She could almost taste the bloodlust.

And when she felt those dark stirrings, she came back to the same question. Could a place drive a man to kill? Was that why the women twenty years ago had been murdered in Moriah's Landing? Was that why poor Claire had been tortured?

Was that why Bethany Peters lay stone-cold in a mortuary cooler?

A frigid blast of air encompassed Elizabeth as she opened the cooler door. The unit was equipped with two removable trays, one on top of the other, so that bodies, or even gurneys and caskets, could be slid in and out without much effort. Bethany had been placed on the top tray, her features frozen in death, her face bluish in the gleam of the flashlight. She looked pale and perfect, almost ethereally beautiful.

As Elizabeth placed her hand on the tray and slid it out, something moved in the darkness behind her. A rustle. A tiny whisper of noise that could have been nothing more than imagination.

But a finger of dread slipped up her backbone.

She turned, playing the flashlight over the room once again. In a far corner, almost concealed by shadow, a gurney covered with a sheet had been shoved against the wall. The white cloth molded itself to the body that lay beneath it.

The sheet moved.

A pale hand lifted.

And Elizabeth felt her entire body go rigid with fear.

Chapter Five

Elizabeth gasped and jumped back, smashing into the cooler with a hard thud. The flashlight slipped from her fingers and crashed to the floor. The bulb flickered, then went out, plunging the room into total darkness.

Heart knocking, Elizabeth kept her gaze fixed on the spot where she'd last seen the gurney. She could see nothing. Could hear nothing but the sound of her own pulse roaring in her ears.

But she knew she wasn't alone.

The air around her seemed to shift and quiver with an unknown presence, a malevolent entity that watched and waited. Elizabeth could feel those invisible eyes on her in the darkness.

Cold air from the open cooler whispered along her backbone as she pressed herself against the metal. For a moment, nothing happened. All was silent. And then in a flurry of movement, someone—*something*—rushed toward her in the blackness.

Elizabeth screamed and tried to move out of the way, but the gurney caught her in the midsection, knocking the breath from her lungs as she slammed backward into the cooler.

She dropped to the floor, banging her head on the metal tray as she fell. In a daze, she heard footsteps scurry across the tile. The door opened into the receiving area and light seeped in for just a split second before the door closed behind an escaping form. Then all was quiet again. All was pitch-black.

Elizabeth shoved the gurney out of her way. Groaning, she tried to get up, but something rested on her shoulder, holding her down. She lifted her hand, felt cold flesh. Dead flesh. Bethany's arm had dropped over the side of the tray and her hand had come to rest on Elizabeth's shoulder.

Scrambling away, Elizabeth managed to rise on shaky legs just as the light came on in the cooler room. The sudden brilliance blinded her, disoriented her, and for one terror-stricken moment, she thought the intruder was coming back to finish her off. Her mouth went dry with fear as she watched the door slowly open, and then a dark figure stepped into the room.

Elizabeth collapsed against the wall, her breath almost a sob. "Cullen!"

His gaze widened when he saw her. He glanced at her, the open cooler, then back at her. "What the hell are you doing here?" he demanded.

He must have seen then that something was very wrong because he strode across the room and took her arm. In spite of the lingering shock and the protection of her velvet cloak, Elizabeth's skin tingled all the way up to her shoulder.

"What happened? Are you all right?"

"I'm fine." But her voice sounded as unsteady as her legs felt. "Someone was in here, Cullen. He shoved the gurney against me and—"

"Wait a minute," Cullen said grimly. "What are *you* doing in here?"

She gave him a weak shrug. "Never mind that now. I'll explain everything later, but we have to see if we can find who was in here. It might have been the killer—" She broke off when she spotted something lying on the floor. "What's that?"

Cullen glanced in the direction she indicated. He walked over and bent down. "Looks like a test tube."

Elizabeth came to stand above him. The empty glass vial was about four inches long and three-quarters of an inch in diameter, capped with a rubber stopper.

"Cullen!" In her excitement, Elizabeth placed her hand on his shoulder, then immediately removed it. "Whoever was in here must have dropped it."

"You don't know that. Someone on the mortuary staff could have left it."

"But you are going to send it to the lab, right?"

No sooner had the words left her mouth than she saw what Cullen was doing. He'd withdrawn an evidence bag from his coat pocket, and using his pen, expertly flipped the vial into the bag without touching the glass.

"If it *doesn't* belong to the mortuary staff, then why would someone bring a test tube into the cooler room?" Elizabeth mused.

Cullen stood. "I don't know," he said in a strange voice. "Why don't you tell me?"

His words took a moment to sink in. Then Elizabeth put a hand to her chest in outrage. "You think *I* brought it? That's ridiculous!"

He gave her a shrewd appraisal. "Is it? Why are you here?"

She glared up at him. "I can't believe you're standing here interrogating me when whoever was in this room might still be in the funeral home. He's the one who can give you answers."

"Come on." Cullen took her arm.

"What? Wait a minute." Elizabeth tried to pull back. "Did you hear what I said? The killer could be in the funeral home at this very moment. We have to search it—"

"*We* don't have to do a damn thing," Cullen said through gritted teeth. "I can't believe you, Elizabeth. What the hell were you thinking? Don't you realize you may have just tainted evidence?"

By this time they were at the door. He opened it and pulled her through, then drew her across the receiving area to the back door. Freezing air cut through Elizabeth's wrap as they hurried outside. A squad car was parked in the drive near the back door, and she could see an officer sitting behind the wheel. When he spotted Cullen, he opened the door and got out.

"Detective Ryan? Everything okay?"

Cullen gripped Elizabeth's elbow. "There may be an intruder in the funeral home, Dewey. Go around and cover the front while I have a look around here."

Officer Dewey glanced briefly at Elizabeth, nodded, and then took off.

Cullen opened the back door of the squad car and all but shoved her inside. For a moment, she tried to struggle away from him. Then she had to wrestle with her skirts, and by that time, Cullen had the situation well under control.

He leaned down, peering at her inside the car. "I'll deal with you later. Right now, I'm locking you inside."

Elizabeth tried to muster a little dignity. "You can't do tha—"

The door slammed closed and Cullen disappeared back into the funeral home.

Elizabeth reached for the door handle, but, of course, there wasn't one. A wire mesh screen separated the back seat from the rest of the car, and she suddenly realized how helpless prisoners must feel, trapped inside with no way out. But there was one big difference in their plight and hers. She was innocent. She'd done nothing but try to help, and this was the thanks she got?

On the second story, lights came on in Ned Krauter's residence. Then one by one, lights came on in the ground-floor windows as Cullen and Officer Dewey searched the premises. The third floor remained dark, which somehow seemed ominous to Elizabeth.

Several minutes passed before Cullen finally came back outside. Elizabeth was freezing by this time. She huddled inside her cloak, teeth chattering, as she watched Cullen and Officer Dewey speak in low tones just outside the squad car. She pressed her ear to the glass, but she couldn't hear a word they were saying. For a moment, she thought Cullen might have forgotten about her, and she considered rapping on the window to draw his attention. As if sensing her intention, he deliberately turned his back on her.

Elizabeth sat back against the seat, fuming. Smarting.

Finally, the door opened and he leaned down. "You okay in there?"

As if he cared. "I'm fine." Elizabeth slanted him a sullen glance. "Did you find anything?"

"No."

"What about the third floor?"

"Krauter said it's rented to a fisherman, named Cross. Krauter says his boat went out a few days ago. Without a warrant we can't search his place, and without probable cause, which we don't have, we're not likely to get a judge this time of night to sign one. But the door was locked. No way the intruder could have gotten in."

"What about the first floor? The chapel—"

"We searched the damn place from top to bottom, okay? If someone was in there, he managed to get away—"

"Wait a minute," Elizabeth said sharply. "If? *If?* There *was* someone in the cooler room. I saw him."

"Did you recognize him? Can you give me a description?"

"No…"

"Why not?"

"I didn't actually *see* him," Elizabeth admitted. "He was hiding underneath a sheet on the gurney. When I saw the sheet move, it—it startled me, and I dropped my flashlight. The light went out so I didn't see who it was. But there might be fingerprints on the test tube. Or on the gurney. He shoved it into me."

"You keep saying he."

She gave a helpless gesture with her hand. "Whoever it was." When he didn't say anything for a moment, Elizabeth peered up at him. "You believe me, don't you?"

"I'm sure you think you saw someone," he said carefully.

Her eyes widened in indignation. "I *did* see someone. Why would I lie about something like that?"

"I'm not accusing you of lying." Cullen raked his hand through his short hair, spiking it even more. His breath frosted in the cold air. "Look, you were alone inside a mortuary cooler room with a corpse. Considering everything, it's no wonder you were scared."

"I never said I was scared. And considering what things?"

"You're young. Impressionable. And after finding the body earlier—"

"I didn't imagine the test tube, did I?" Elizabeth demanded, anger flushing her face. "I'm telling you, someone was in that room with me!"

Cullen's gaze on her hardened. "Which brings us back to my original question. What were *you* doing in there?"

Elizabeth stared straight ahead, refusing to meet his gaze. "I told you earlier I wanted to have a closer look at the body."

"And I told you to stay out of it. I could haul you in for interfering in an official investigation. Maybe even slap an obstruction of justice charge on you."

She glanced at him then. "You wouldn't."

He shrugged. "Not this time. But I'm warning you. I'm losing my patience. I can't have you running around tampering with evidence. When I make an arrest in this case, I don't want the suspect waltzing out of it on some legal technicality. You got that?"

"Yes, I've got it." With an effort, she tried to regain her calm. "Look, I know you don't have any faith in my ability. You've made that perfectly clear. But I'm not just some...cop groupie here. I have a lot of training, Cullen. I could help you solve this case if you'd let me."

"And I told you if I need your help, I'll ask for it. Did you hear me asking?"

She lifted her chin but said nothing.

"Well, did you?"

"No," she replied grudgingly. "But I meant what I said, too. I saw something on that body. I don't know what. I can't put my finger on it. But something…bothered me. And my intuition is rarely wrong."

"Your intuition?"

"Yes. You know—"

"Spare me the dictionary definition. I know what it means, I just don't put much stock in it."

"You don't have instincts? You don't get a gut feeling about certain cases?"

"Sometimes," he admitted. "But my gut feelings are based on training and experience. Not on some whim."

Elizabeth shook her head. "You just can't admit it, can you?"

"Admit what?"

"That I might be your equal. In training and experience."

"Lecturing in a classroom is a lot different than running a criminal investigation. When you've put your time in on the street, then we'll talk." Cullen straightened. "In the meantime, I'm going to drive you home."

He put out a hand to help her from the car, but Elizabeth ignored it. Again she struggled with the folds of her costume, but finally managed to crawl from the back seat with a modicum of poise. "I don't need a ride," she said coolly. "I have my own car."

"You may not need a ride, but you've got one

anyway.'' He took her arm firmly and steered her toward a dark, plain sedan parked behind the squad car. ''I'll drive you myself so I can make sure you get there.''

''What about my car?''

''You can pick it up tomorrow.''

Elizabeth started to protest about leaving her new car parked on the street, but considering all that she'd witnessed that night, it seemed a little petty to worry about vandalism.

THEY'D BEEN DRIVING in silence for several minutes when Cullen finally gave her a bemused glance. ''By the way, I've been meaning to ask you all night. What the hell is that getup you're wearing?''

''This?'' Elizabeth lifted one of the velvety folds of her wrap. ''It's called a cloak. It's part of my costume.''

''Which is?''

She opened her mouth to answer, but as she turned to face him, the words froze on her lips. In the dim light from the dash, Cullen's features were shadowy, indistinct. Dressed all in black, he reminded her of a dark angel, a shadow hero, a complicated man with complicated motives.

It suddenly occurred to Elizabeth that she actually knew very little about Cullen Ryan. She'd had a crush on him for years, but she didn't really know who he was or what made him tick.

Oh, she knew *some* things about him. He'd grown up down by the docks, and he'd gotten into some trouble as a teenager. His father had died after Cullen had left for Boston, and she didn't think he had any other family in Moriah's Landing. So what had brought him back here?

Why return to a place that hadn't been all that kind to him?

The only thing Elizabeth knew for certain about Cullen was that he'd left town a juvenile delinquent and returned a cop, one with dark secrets and a troubled past. What had happened in those six years to change him?

Or had he changed?

Were the demons that had driven him to mischief as a boy still driving him today as a man? Was his becoming a cop an attempt to control those darker impulses?

Elizabeth shuddered at the thought. At his nearness.

In response, Cullen reached up and pounded the dash with his fist. "Sorry. Heater doesn't work like it should."

There was plenty of heat inside that car. Or at least, the potential for it. "I'm fine," she managed.

"So what did you say you went as tonight?" His gaze swept over her cloak.

"A noblewoman," Elizabeth murmured. "Seventeenth-century."

"Figures," he muttered.

"What?"

"Nothing."

They were cruising down Main Street now, nearing the turn that would have taken them to the Pierce compound. The rain had stopped, and a pre-dawn mist had settled over the town, creeping like a ghost along the cobblestone walkways. A variety of businesses, some of them housed in tall, narrow buildings that were centuries-old, crowded the thoroughfare, their windows dark at this hour, their doorways steeped in shadow.

As in Salem, some of the enterprises had capitalized on the history of Moriah's Landing. Witches rode weathervanes mounted high on gable rooftops, while black metal cats with green marble eyes slumbered a few feet away on brick chimneys. A souvenir shop, squeezed between a dusty apothecary and an antiques store, sold everything from spell books to T-shirts emblazoned with McFarland Leary's image—or what an artist had perceived as his likeness. Another shop offered midnight ghost tours.

It was harmless, this exploitation of the town's past to draw in tourists, especially in the fall during the Halloween celebrations. The locals were proud of their heritage, and even though they were a superstitious lot, they didn't mind using the legends to make a buck. Most hadn't even resisted when a group of nature-loving Wiccans had proclaimed Moriah's Landing their spiritual epicenter and had camped out for weeks on end near Raven's Cove, performing midnight rituals and dancing naked under a full moon—or so some said.

It was all harmless....

But Elizabeth had never quite been able to get into the spirit of the celebrations because, in spite of the town's rich history and unique charm, she'd sensed, from an early age, a darkness lingering in murky alleys, crouching in recessed doorways. A malicious presence that hid from the light and preyed on the innocent. She stayed on in the town because of her family, and because the darkness fascinated her as much as it repelled her.

Shivering, she averted her eyes from those door-ways.

But they were driving by the town green now, a heavily landscaped area where, according to lore, those accused of practicing witchcraft in the late 1600s had been hung from the gnarled branches of an old oak tree. A plaque commemorated the spot, and the townspeople had come to think of the ground beneath the tree limbs as hallowed.

Whether the legend was true or not, Elizabeth didn't know. But of all the places in Moriah's Landing, the town green, particularly the oak tree, still standing, seemed to elicit the strongest feelings in her, an inexplicable sensation that evil lurked nearby. That it watched her every move. That if she wasn't very careful, she could be its next victim.

She clenched her fists and squeezed her eyes closed as they passed by the tree. In her mind's eye, she could see a crowd milling about on the square, their clothing and expressions somber, their eyes turned skyward.

Elizabeth's imagination followed their stares.

She could see feet dangling among the leaves, and as her gaze moved upward, she saw Bethany Peters's pale face staring down at her.

Heart pounding, she opened her eyes, dispelling the vision. Bethany Peters hadn't really been hanging from the same tree where witches had been killed centuries ago. Elizabeth's imagination was playing tricks on her. It was silly to be upset by a vision, especially after everything else she'd been through that night.

Still…

She couldn't shake that tenacious unease that

something watched her. That something waited for her.

That whoever or whatever had killed Bethany had some kind of connection to Elizabeth.

First Claire, then Tasha.

And now one of Elizabeth's students.

You're next, a dark voice seemed to whisper.

Chapter Six

As the town green receded, the tension slowly drained from Elizabeth, and she began to breathe much more easily.

Heathrow College lay just ahead, a private institution safely ensconced behind a high stone wall broken only by an electronically-controlled gate that was monitored twenty-four hours a day by a security guard. The parents who were willing to pay the steep tuition at the exclusive school wanted more than just the finest education for their daughters. They wanted assurances that the young women would be safe, tucked away from the real world and protected by state-of-the-art security equipment.

Some of the girls rebelled at the school's rigid rules and outdated curfew, much as Elizabeth had once done herself at boarding school. But for some reason, she'd never found Heathrow confining—as a student or as a member of the faculty—perhaps because coming here had been her choice.

Although it wasn't so much a choice as a need, she realized. A need for independence. A need to become her own person. A need to get away from the disappointment that was all too apparent in her parents' eyes every time they looked at her.

She'd had such potential, their expressions seemed to reproach her. How had she gone so far astray?

Elizabeth had known from an early age that she was expected to follow in her parents' illustrious footsteps. Marion and Edward Douglas were brilliant, renowned scientists who'd made their mark in research long before they'd turned thirty—her mother in genetics, her father in the related field of molecular biology.

They'd met at Harvard, fallen in love, married and had a baby, all in the space of a year, which had always seemed so out of character for them to Elizabeth. She found it almost impossible to imagine that her parents—so serious now, so single-minded—had once been young and in love. For as long as she could remember, their work had consumed them, and nothing, not their love affair and certainly not their daughter, had been allowed to interfere.

They'd both eventually left their affiliation with Harvard to join a private research lab in Boston to which they commuted at least five days a week and sometimes seven. Their only concession to their parental obligations was to buy a beautiful home in Moriah's Landing, furnish it elegantly, and hire a full-time nanny for Elizabeth until she was old enough to be shipped off to boarding school, the same prestigious institution her mother had attended.

But Elizabeth was not at all like her mother, and she'd rebelled against the pressures and expectations placed on her because of her heritage and her IQ. She'd hated boarding school with a passion, and by the time she turned ten had run away numerous times.

Finally, after a frantic call from the school director, her parents had been forced to deal with her. If they sent her back to that place, she'd told them, she would just keep running away until the school was finally obliged to expel her. If they sent her to another boarding school, she would do the same thing. And one day, she might never come back.

At their wits' end, her parents had finally allowed her to return to Moriah's Landing and attend public school on two conditions: one, that she enroll in a grade well above her peer group, and, two, that she supplement her studies by simultaneously taking courses at Heathrow.

As a result, Elizabeth had graduated from high school at the age of fifteen, and when she enrolled full-time at Heathrow, she'd already earned enough credits for undergraduate degrees in both math and biology.

But after Claire had been abducted, Elizabeth had switched her field of study to criminology. That had been the last straw as far as her parents were concerned. They'd washed their hands of her and turned their attention in the last year or so to Elizabeth's younger brother, Brandon, who, at four, showed signs of a genius that far outclassed Elizabeth's. He had already been accepted to the most prestigious school in the northeast, where he would be sent when he turned six. Just two years away.

The thought of her little brother being sent to live among strangers, his young mind and imagination molded by the same robotic teachers who'd tried to constrain hers made Elizabeth almost physically ill, made her want to take him somewhere far away where he wouldn't be subjected to the same killing loneliness she'd known as a child.

It was a cliché, Elizabeth knew, but her parents had never understood her, never appreciated the fact that she marched to a different drummer. They didn't get that she had needs apart from their own, needs above and beyond the classroom and research lab. She had a fine mind, yes, but she also had a heart. She also had the same wants and desires that any twenty-year-old had. That they, themselves, had once had and lost.

Elizabeth turned slightly, studying Cullen's profile. Sometimes she wondered if her attraction to him was yet another rebellion against her parents. If she would wake up one day to find that she'd spent a good portion of her youth pining for a man who didn't really exist except in her dreams. Because the real Cullen Ryan couldn't possibly live up to her fantasies. No man could.

He turned suddenly, capturing her with a gaze so dark, so intense, Elizabeth caught her breath. Her stomach quivered with awareness, with attraction, and she realized that whatever the reason for her fascination with Cullen, it was only growing more potent as she spent time with him.

"What?" he asked with a scowl.

"What what?" she managed to stammer.

"Why are you looking at me like that?"

"Because..." She fumbled for an answer. "I was just wondering.... You said you sometimes get a gut feeling about a case based on your training and experience. What do you think about this one?"

He hesitated just a fraction too long. "I don't like to speculate."

Elizabeth glanced at him. "You found something, didn't you?"

"I'm not going to discuss the specifics of this case with you, Elizabeth."

She sighed. "But don't you find it strange there were no visible marks on her body? It was almost as if the killer went out of his way to…preserve her."

"You're making a pretty big assumption there."

"I'm not assuming anything, I'm just thinking out loud." Elizabeth paused. "Can you at least tell me if you think there's a possibility that Bethany's killer is the same one who murdered those women here twenty years ago?"

He looked surprised. "Why do you ask that?"

She stared out the windshield, noticing how the mist writhed and curled in the headlights. "It's hard to imagine a town the size of Moriah's Landing falling prey to more than one serial killer."

"Whoa. Slow down." He shot her a frowning glance. "One murder doesn't make a serial killer. I don't want talk like that getting out. Besides, twenty years is a long time for a predator to remain active."

"Not if he was incarcerated during that time. Or if he widened his hunting ground. All I'm saying is that twenty years ago, four young women were murdered in Moriah's Landing. Five years ago, a friend of mine was abducted and tortured, and I think she would have been killed, too, if she hadn't managed to escape. And now this. I can't help wondering if all the crimes could be related."

"Those women's bodies were dumped," Cullen pointed out. "They weren't hanged."

"I realize that, but there could be another kind of

connection. Do you think it's possible—'' She broke off, biting her lip.

"What?"

"Nothing."

"No, tell me what you were about to say."

"You'd just think I'm crazy. Or young. Or that I'm letting my imagination run away with me." Elizabeth felt his gaze on her, and reluctantly she turned to face him.

He glanced at the road, then back at her, his gaze deep, probing. Sensuous, even though she was quite certain he didn't mean for it to be. Not with her.

But the term *bedroom eyes* had never been more appropriate. Elizabeth couldn't see his eyes clearly in the dash lights, but she knew they were a stony gray rimmed with darkness. His pupils were small, giving him a piercing, unearthly quality that seemed capable of penetrating a woman's soul.

"All right," she said nervously. "But please promise me you won't laugh."

He shrugged, refusing to commit himself one way or the other.

She drew a breath. "Sometimes I can't help wondering if this place, this town drives people to violence, if something from the past, something…evil resides here."

Cullen stared at her for a moment, then shifted his focus back to the road. To his credit, he didn't laugh. He didn't even appear amused. But he wasn't buying her theory. "A place doesn't kill. People kill."

"I know, but—"

He did laugh then, a low, throaty chuckle that sent a warm thrill up Elizabeth's backbone. "Don't tell me you've bought into all those old stories. Someone with your brains? I'm surprised."

She shrugged. "I'm smart enough to know there are things in this world that can't be explained."

"There are things in this world that haven't been explained yet," he said. "Big difference."

Face it, Elizabeth thought. She and Cullen were probably never going to see eye-to-eye on this particular subject. He was too pragmatic, but she wasn't surprised by his attitude. She'd faced the same skepticism from her parents any time she'd tried to broach the subject of the supernatural with them.

After a moment, Cullen said, "That friend you were talking about earlier. Was it Claire Cavendish?"

"How did you know?" Elizabeth asked in surprise. "You'd already left town when she was abducted."

Cullen studied the road. "I must have heard about it somewhere. I seem to recall something about a sorority initiation." He glanced at her expectantly. "You were there, weren't you?"

Elizabeth nodded, a lump forming in her throat. She still had a hard time talking about that night. "Yes, I was there."

"What happened?"

"Why do you want to know?"

He shrugged. "Because, on the slight chance that you're right and there is a connection to this latest murder, I'll need to know anything you can tell me about what happened to her." When Elizabeth remained silent, he said, "You did say you wanted to help, right?"

He would use that against her. Elizabeth folded her arms and turned to stare out the window. After a moment, she said, "There were five of us that night. Kat

Ridgemont, Tasha Pierce, Brie Dudley, Claire and myself. We were supposed to camp out in St. John's Cemetery near McFarland Leary's grave, and one of us had to spend part of the night alone in the old haunted mausoleum.''

Elizabeth shivered though it was quite warm inside the car. "It was a bad idea from the start. Hazing had been banned by the college and by all the sororities years ago, but this particular sorority had a set of secret rules that pertained only to the local students who wanted to join. Most of the girls came from Boston and New York. Those of us from Moriah's Landing had to prove ourselves worthy. And we didn't really object. Not at first. We just thought of it as an adventure. All of us except Claire. She was scared even before we got to the cemetery, but she really wanted to be accepted by the sorority. She was afraid if we didn't go through with the initiation, one or all of us would be blackballed.''

"What happened when you got to the cemetery?"

"A storm was about to hit. I remember the flashes of lightning in the distance, and the wind. There was a moon, but heavy clouds blocked most of the light. We had to use flashlights to locate Leary's grave, and then we drew lots to see who would have to spend the night in the mausoleum. Claire lost. We all told her she didn't have to do it, that we didn't care whether the sorority blackballed us or not, but she insisted she wanted to go through with it.

"When she disappeared inside the crypt, the rest of us gathered in a circle around the grave, joining hands to form a protective circle to keep out evil—''

Cullen threw her a startled glance. "You *what?*"

Elizabeth's face burned with embarrassment. She

hadn't really meant to tell him about that part. She'd never told anyone about the spell. Not her parents, not the police, not anyone. She and the other girls had never spoken of it again. For one thing, there were too many people in town who wouldn't understand. For another, there were too many people in town who *would*.

She said in a rush, "Like I said, it was all supposed to be harmless. Then we heard Claire scream. By the time we got the door of the mausoleum open, she was gone. Vanished without a trace."

Cullen said grimly, "What do you mean without a trace? The police found nothing?"

"No."

"And you and the others didn't see anything? Didn't hear anything? How far away from the crypt were you?"

"Maybe ten yards."

"And someone got inside, took Claire, and no one saw or heard anything?"

Elizabeth detected the skepticism in his voice, and suddenly she was transported back to that night. Back to the terror. The awful guilt. The suspicion gleaming in the eyes of the police officers who'd questioned her.

That suspicion hadn't gone away for a very long time, and neither had the guilt. And now Cullen was making her live it all over again. The one person whose trust meant more than anything to Elizabeth was looking at her as if he didn't believe her.

She said defensively, "I don't know how it happened. Or why. But Claire has never been the same since."

Cullen threw her a careful glance. "What exactly was done to her?"

"We...never knew the details. The police withheld the information, partly for her sake, and I think partly because they still suspected one or all of us may have been involved. I think for a while they were hoping one of us would slip up."

"So you don't know the extent of her injuries?"

Elizabeth shook her head. "All we were ever told was that she was tortured before she managed to escape from her kidnapper, and her mind just shut down. When she was found in the cemetery a few days later, she couldn't tell anyone where she'd been or who had taken her, let alone what was done to her. After that, her mother whisked her off to a private institution in another town. She's been there ever since."

"Can she have visitors?"

Elizabeth turned. "Why?"

"Because if you're right and her abduction is connected to Bethany Peters's murder, then I'm going to need to talk to her."

"It's no use. You'd be wasting your time. She can't tell you anything."

He lifted a brow. "Can't or won't?"

"Can't."

"Maybe you're right, then. Maybe I would be wasting my time." He pulled the car to a stop outside the electronic gate at Heathrow. Flushed from his warm station, George, the guard, hurried over to the car with an impatient scowl, but instead of lowering the window, Cullen turned back to Elizabeth. "If it's all the same with you, though, I'd like to try talking to her anyway."

Elizabeth frowned. "Why? You said yourself you don't really think the crimes are connected."

He gave her a ghost of a smile. "Let's just say, you have me intrigued."

Elizabeth's heart pounded against her rib cage at the look he gave her. At the way he leaned slightly toward her. With very little effort, she could lift her hand to his face, stroke her fingers along his cheek, trace the outline of his jaw, his chin, his lips. With even less effort, she could touch her mouth to his....

She glanced at George outside the window. He was peering in intently.

"I wouldn't want you to upset her," she said in a breathless half-whisper. "She's been through so much. If you start talking about that night—"

Cullen cocked his head. "What? She might remember something?" He stared at Elizabeth for a long, tense moment, ignoring the rap of George's knuckle on the window, the glare of his flashlight beam. "Why do I get the feeling there's something you aren't telling me about that night?"

"There isn't."

"No?" His gaze slipped over her. "Then why are you trembling, Elizabeth?"

SURROUNDED by a low stone wall, Elizabeth's cottage—one of several residences granted by the college for some of the faculty members—was almost hidden from view by a thick stand of oak and maple trees that provided thick shade in the summer and a dazzling display of color in autumn. In the winter, however, the trees looked skeletal, desolate and not a little eerie with mist curling like smoke around their bases.

The house was small, a one-bedroom with a steeply pitched gable roof and diamond-paned casement windows that were in perfect keeping with the local architecture. The only access was by cobblestone walkways that connected the residential area to the rest of the campus. A faculty parking lot was provided nearby, and as Cullen pulled into a space, Elizabeth was surprised when he shut off the engine. She'd been certain he would let her out as quickly as possible.

He opened the door, and a wintry blast gusted through the car. "I'll see you home."

"You don't have to do that." Elizabeth was suddenly nervous. "It's not far, and the campus is perfectly safe."

But was it? Bethany Peters had been a student at Heathrow, and although her body hadn't been found on campus, they didn't yet know where she'd been killed. Or who her murderer was. Or if, in fact, there might be some connection to the college.

Elizabeth had always felt safe behind those lichen-covered walls, but now she realized that the elaborate security precautions were hardly more than an illusion. If someone wanted in badly enough, the walls could be scaled. The gate could be short-circuited. The guard could be fooled.

The murderer could even be someone who lived behind those walls....

Cullen came around and opened her door, reaching out a hand to help her from the car. If he noticed how badly her hand shook, he said nothing.

Climbing out of the car, Elizabeth patted down the folds of her heavy cloak and the swirling hoops of her skirt. "I don't know how women used to manage,'' she muttered, trying to alleviate the fear that had suddenly gripped her.

"That is some outfit," he agreed.

For a moment, their gazes met, and in the light from a street lamp, Elizabeth saw amusement spark in Cullen's dark gaze. Amusement...and something else. Or was that, too, her imagination?

A tremor slowly rolled along her nerve endings.

"This way," she said breathlessly and started down the walkway to her home.

The campus slumbered unaware. In the distance, an occasional light glinted from a dorm window where an unfortunate student was having to pull an all-nighter. Or more likely, where a late-night drinking party and gabfest was taking place. In a little while, Bethany's room would be roped off with police tape, and word of her murder would be all over school. Elizabeth could already feel a funereal pall settling over the campus.

She turned up her walkway, pausing at her front door. "Well, this is it." She stared up at Cullen. "Thanks for walking me home."

"I'll see you inside."

Elizabeth's heart gave a funny little trip. Alone with Cullen in the close confines of her house? How was she going to handle that? What was she going to say to him?

She had a feeling small talk wasn't going to be a problem. Undoubtedly, the only reason he lingered was to lecture her again.

I'm warning you, Elizabeth.

I'm losing my patience with you, Elizabeth.

Don't go playing Nancy Drew with my case, Elizabeth.

Bracing herself for his complaints, she unlocked her door and walked inside. She'd left a lamp burning earlier, and now, after such a night, her diminutive living quarters were even more of a welcome sight than usual. She closed the door behind Cullen, then turned, surveying the room with a quick, critical sweep, wondering what he would see, what he would think of her home. What it might reveal, inadvertently, about herself.

The area was crowded with furniture—refinished antiques, tall bookcases, deep tufted sofas and chairs where she could curl up in front of the stone fireplace at night or on a rainy day and read a good book. The floors were maple, stained a golden hue that was a welcome contrast to the darker, heavier pieces of furniture.

On the walls, she'd mounted old photographs and newspaper articles collected from area flea markets and antique shops which provided a rich cornucopia of the town's history dating back over two hundred years. The earlier annals of Moriah's Landing, including the witch trials of the late 1600s, were retold in dozens of leather-bound tomes she kept under lock and key—along with some of her other prized volumes—in an old scarred armoire in the bedroom.

She turned expectantly to Cullen.

"It's chilly in here," he said with a frown. "Do you want me to start you a fire?"

Did she want him to start her a fire?

She'd wanted that for a very long time.

"Yes, thank you," she murmured. "I'll make some tea."

Hurrying into the tiny kitchen, Elizabeth leaned against the doorframe for a moment as she tried to catch her breath. She'd been dreaming of this moment for years. She finally had Cullen Ryan alone in her home. She was making tea while he built a fire. It all seemed so cozy. So...domestic. Perhaps they could snuggle up in front of the flames and sip their tea, and then later—

"Elizabeth? Better make that tea quick. I can't stay long. I have to get back."

The romantic record on Elizabeth's imaginary phonograph scratched to a halt.

So much for later, she thought as she put the kettle on the stove.

While she waited for the water to boil, she slipped out of her cloak, and using the tiny washroom off the kitchen, tried to tidy her hair. She'd had it styled that afternoon at Chops, the best salon in town, but the elaborate updo had come loose in places, and tendrils fell about her shoulders in hopeless disarray. Nothing short of brushing the whole thing out completely would help, but Elizabeth didn't have time for that. She removed a few hairpins, gave her head a good toss, and then shrugged. That was the best she could do.

Arranging cups and a teapot on a tray, she carried everything into the living room and placed them on a low table near the fireplace where a blaze crackled and hissed pleasantly in the silence.

Cullen, studying some of the photographs she'd exhibited on the walls, didn't turn immediately when she came in.

Elizabeth bent over the tray to pour the tea. "How do you take your tea?"

When he didn't answer, she glanced up, thinking

perhaps he hadn't heard her. But his attention was riveted on her. Or rather, on her chest.

Elizabeth glanced down and almost gasped. Somehow the WonderBra had shifted during the evening's activities, and now instead of pushing her together and up, it was pushing her together, up and out. She looked as if she were about to pop over the daring neckline of her dress, and Elizabeth had never popped over anything.

Her face went red-hot.

Her first instinct was to adjust the bra or tug on her neckline. Instead she straightened, trying to act cavalierly about the whole affair. But then she caught a glimpse of herself in a wall mirror behind Cullen, and she was even more shocked by the amount of cleavage she'd put on display. Had her chest been that prominent all evening? No one else had seemed to notice.

But Cullen was sure noticing. He couldn't seem to tear his gaze from her décolletage, and, in her nervousness, Elizabeth drew a deep breath, which only accentuated the problem.

Slowly, Cullen looked up. Something glinted in his eyes, something warm and dark. Something that made Elizabeth's stomach tremble and her knees go weak.

"Tea?" Her voice came out hardly more than a croak. Cullen seemed startled by the sound of it. Or at least, *something* had jolted him.

He gazed at her as if he didn't quite comprehend. "What? Oh, tea. No. Sorry. I'd better pass. I need to get back...." He was backing toward the front door, all but stumbling in his haste.

Elizabeth started toward him. "Are you sure?"

He put up a hand. "Yes. Very sure." He bumped

into a chair. "It's late and you need to get some breast—*rest*." He opened the door and retreated outside. "Good night, Elizabeth."

"Good night, Cullen."

She watched him stride down the walkway toward the parking lot. Once he was out of sight, Elizabeth turned and leaned against the door, hugging her middle.

And then she smiled.

She couldn't believe it! She'd actually made him nervous! *She!* Geeky little Elizabeth Douglas. Who would have thought?

Who would have thought that with all her years of studying, all her degrees, all her brain power, what she'd really needed to get Cullen Ryan's attention was a good push-up bra?

Chapter Seven

In spite of an almost sleepless night, Elizabeth rose early the next morning, showered, dressed and downed a bagel and two cups of coffee before leaving to meet Lucian LeCroix at the library.

The sun was shining when she walked outside, but the temperature had dropped during the early morning hours and a sharp wind blew out of the northeast. Icicles suspended from barren tree limbs glinted like diamonds in the early-morning light, but the effect was more depressing than beautiful to Elizabeth. The cold reminded her of death, and death reminded her of Bethany's murder and the fact that her killer was still out there somewhere, perhaps even now searching for his next victim.

As she hurried along, Elizabeth resisted the urge to glance over her shoulder. It was broad daylight, but the campus was almost deserted. She met only a handful of students on the walkway, their heads bowed against the biting wind. As Elizabeth neared the library, two girls from one of her classes recognized her and called out a greeting. Another waved from a ten-speed as she pedaled by, her breath steaming like a racehorse's in the cold.

In all likelihood, the students Elizabeth encountered were only a year or two younger than she. Some of them might even have been older, but their faces all looked so fresh and earnest. So innocent.

Had they heard about Bethany?

Even for those girls who didn't know her personally, news of her death would still come as a shock. A stunned disbelief would descend over the campus, and then, as details of the murder trickled out, imaginations would be fueled. Rumors would spread like wildfire. Human nature being what it was, the more grisly aspects of Bethany's death would eventually enthrall as much as they would terrify.

Elizabeth thought about Bethany lying in the cooler, her skin tinted that awful bluish-gray death hue, her eyes open and staring, but not seeing as she waited for the pathologist's scalpels and saws. Just a few short days ago she'd been like the other girls at Heathrow. Young, vibrant, her whole life ahead of her. Now that life had been cut short, snuffed out by a brutal killer driven by passions so dark and hideous that no one but he could fathom them.

Passions that would have to be sated time and time again.

She was guessing at the killer's motives, of course, and she could be wrong. Elizabeth *hoped* she was wrong. She prayed that Bethany's murder, as tragic as it would still be, had been committed by a crazed boyfriend. A jilted lover. A jealous rival. Anything but what Elizabeth feared most.

She remembered what Cullen had told her last night. *One murder doesn't make a serial killer.... Besides, twenty years is a long time for a predator to remain active.*

Not if he was smart.

Not if his bloodlust was matched by his brilliance, by a cleverness and skill that never let him lose control completely. That never allowed him to become reckless.

Most serial killers considered themselves superior and invincible, but supposing *this* killer really was? What if they were dealing with an extraordinary mind, one that had been carefully cultivated and nurtured until nothing remained but pure cunning? Pure evil?

She gazed into the distance, not seeing David Bryson's castle, but knowing it was there. Knowing he was inside, stalking those dark halls like an animal trapped in a cage.

Could the townspeople be right? Had he killed those women twenty years ago?

A young man at the time, he'd been brought in for questioning, but nothing had ever been proven. And now he had enough money to protect himself. He was even a benefactor of this very college.

But supposing he *had* killed those women. Supposing he had somehow managed to keep those dark urges under control all these years until something had once again unleashed the beast in him.

Elizabeth shivered again as she pulled her coat more tightly around her even though she knew it wouldn't help. She'd dressed warmly for her outing with Lucian LeCroix, but her chill came not from the day, but from within.

A deep, impenetrable shadow had crept over her soul, and no warmth or light would be allowed in until Bethany Peters's murderer was found.

LUCIAN WAITED for her outside the library. Dressed elegantly for a Saturday morning in dark slacks and an expensive, tailored overcoat, he stood near the bottom of the steps, his gaze scanning the campus.

Elizabeth wondered what he would think of the faded jeans and scruffy ski jacket she'd donned for the occasion. Her concern had been directed more at the weather than at appearances, obviously, and in that vein, she'd twisted her hair into a loose bun at the back of her neck and pulled a red stocking cap over her ears. She barely resembled the woman he'd met at the ball last evening, and she wasn't at all certain he would remember her.

But he smiled when she approached, and she saw at once that even without the intriguing mask he'd worn last night, there was still an air of mystery about the man.

It was his eyes, she decided. So dark a brown they almost appeared black, and with a kind of simmering intelligence that made one wonder what he was thinking.

Yes, those eyes were definitely the source of his mystery. And a great deal of his attraction, but not all. He was an extremely handsome man, with an angular face highlighted by glossy jet-black hair which he'd combed straight back. He was only about five-ten or so, but he had that look of intense virility, in spite of his sophistication, that made him seem all male.

"Hello," he said, his voice velvety smooth even in the cold.

Elizabeth held up a gloved hand. "Hello. I'm not late, am I?"

"Right on time." He came down a step or two to

join her at the bottom. "I wasn't sure you'd show up at all, though."

"Why not?"

"Because of what happened last night." A shadow moved in his dark eyes. "I heard you were the one who found the body."

"Who told you that?"

He shrugged. "Once the police arrived, word spread quickly among the guests."

"I'm sure it did." Elizabeth gazed out over the frozen campus, thinking again about Bethany. Seeing her body swaying overhead—

"Is something wrong?" he asked.

She drew a breath. "No, I was just...remembering."

His voice lowered with compassion. "It must have been a horrible shock, finding her like that." He paused. "They said there wasn't a mark on her body. How do the police know it was murder? Couldn't it have been suicide?"

"There were...other indications," Elizabeth said, not wishing to elaborate. "It was obvious she was dead before she was hanged."

"I guess that *would* suggest foul play," he agreed.

Elizabeth tried to shrug off the gloom. "I don't want to talk about any of that today. It's a beautiful morning. The sun's shining...." Murder suddenly seemed a long way off. Evil seemed on holiday. "Let's just get on with the tour, shall we?"

His gaze slipped over her. If he found her appearance lacking, he hid his disapproval admirably. In fact—

No. She had to be mistaken about that glint in his eyes. First Cullen, and now Lucian LeCroix? It was too much to think, certainly too much to hope, that two such great-looking men—albeit very different ones—could show even a crumb of interest in her.

But Elizabeth could have sworn she'd seen that same glint in Cullen's gray eyes last night, a hint of something that she very much wanted to believe was attraction. After all these years, he'd finally looked at her as she imagined a man would look at a woman he wanted, as she'd dreamed for a long time that Cullen would gaze at her.

Had she been wrong about that look, though? Had the desire in his eyes been merely an illusion?

Maybe all she'd seen was...surprise. She'd inadvertently shown him an awful lot of cleavage. Cullen had never seen her that way before. It would be perfectly understandable if he'd been taken aback. Shocked, even.

In the cold light of day, that scenario seemed more likely. Especially in view of their history.

"Elizabeth?"

"Hmmm?" She glanced up, remembered suddenly where she was and whom she was with. "Oh, sorry. I was just thinking about...something."

"Are you sure you're up to this?"

"Oh, absolutely. If it's not too cold for you."

He smiled. "Actually, I like the cold."

Elizabeth stared at him for a moment. Wow, she thought absently. He did have a nice smile. A great smile, really. In fact, he was an extraordinary-looking man. He wasn't Cullen, of course, but his undivided attention was flattering, Elizabeth had to admit.

For the first time in her life, she felt the force of her femininity, that subtle shift in the balance of power between the sexes in her favor. If she wasn't careful, it could become an intoxicating sensation, she decided.

"I'm ready if you are," she said.

"In that case, I eagerly place myself in your capable hands."

She laughed a little at his effusive manner. "So, tell me, have you found a place to stay yet? Are you all settled in?" They started down one of the walkways.

"Yes, as a matter of fact, I've rented a charming little place on Raven's Cove. You'll have to come see it some time."

Elizabeth cleared her throat. "That would be...nice." She hurried to change the subject. "The school is quite small, as I'm sure you're aware. We'll just walk around a bit if that's all right with you. There aren't many classes on Saturday, but you can still get a feel for the campus."

They began at the far southwest corner, where the high stone wall was buttressed by a thick forest of hardwoods. Heavy branches drooped low over the wall, providing the more daring and athletic students easy access to the outside world after the hated curfew. From there it was only a short hike to a paved road that would lead them past the pistol range and eventually into downtown, or more likely, to the waterfront, where several bars and clubs operated till dawn.

After Brie had had to leave school during her sophomore year, Kat and Elizabeth had been the only two remaining at Heathrow of the original five friends. Kat, no stranger to adventure, had led Elizabeth on some harrowing escapades of their own via those tree branches.

"Consider this a valuable part of your education," she would tell Elizabeth as they scrambled over the wall. "Something to tell your grandkids about." Usually dressed in black, and sometimes in leather, Kat would always land on her feet on the other side of the wall, ready for just about anything that came their way. Elizabeth would land on her butt more often than not, but no less game for adventure. Kat brought out the devil in her, as one of their professors had told them once, but Elizabeth had long ago decided that was a good thing.

She wondered briefly what Kat would think of her daring foray into the funeral home last night and her brief encounter later with Cullen at her cottage. "You go, girl," she could almost hear Kat encouraging her.

"That's a tantalizing smile, I must say," Lucian commented.

"Oh, I was just remembering my time here as a student," Elizabeth said. "Heathrow College is the first place I ever felt truly at home."

She hadn't meant to reveal something so personal and was thankful Lucian didn't pry. He merely stared down at her and said softly, "It's a nice campus."

"It is," she agreed, in spite of the cloud that had descended since Bethany's death.

Lucian's eyes were very dark in the sunlight. Deep and mysterious. Elizabeth's stomach fluttered in uneasiness. It was broad daylight, but the campus was still almost deserted. Hardly anyone was about, and here she stood with a man she knew nothing about.

And a student had been murdered recently. Her body had just been found last night. By Elizabeth.

Earlier, she'd been flattered by Lucian's attention, but now she merely felt...unsettled. He was older than she, and very smooth. Experienced. She didn't want him thinking the wrong thing about her. She didn't want him thinking she was available.

But you are *available,* a little voice reminded her.

She was, but she didn't want to be.

They'd crossed the campus by this time and were standing in front of the Natasha Pierce Building of Natural Sciences. Elizabeth glanced around, groping for a harmless topic. "This is our newest building, but, as you can see, the architecture blends quite seamlessly with the rest of the campus. It was designed that way, of course."

Lucian read the dedication over one of the entrances. "Pierce, as in our hosts last evening?"

Elizabeth nodded. "Yes. This building was constructed almost entirely through donations made by the Pierce Foundation, which was established years ago by a Pierce ancestor who was also a prominent scientist. The family has maintained close ties to the school since its founding. They named the building after their daughter who died five years ago in a boating accident." Elizabeth started up the steps, shaking off her feelings of sadness at Tasha's memory. "Would you like to look around inside? The Biology Department is first rate, and the new laboratories are state of the art." Plus, what safer—and less romantic—environment than the sterile confines of a lab?

"I've never had much of an interest in science," he admitted with a wry smile. "Dissecting frogs and pig embryos isn't exactly my thing, but I wouldn't mind having a look around." As long as you're with me, his eyes seemed to say.

You're reading too much into this, Elizabeth warned herself as she led the way inside. Lucian was new in town, and she was the first person associated with the school that he'd met last night. He was probably just wanting to be friends.

And she hardly looked glamorous this morning. She was, as she'd always been, just plain Elizabeth Douglas. Smart, yes, and mildly attractive, but nothing to write home about. Not at all the type to inspire a man's romantic fantasies.

Certainly not a man like Lucian LeCroix. Elizabeth could tell just by looking at him that he'd been with lots of women, and he knew exactly how to treat them. How to woo them. How to make them fall at his feet.

A real lady-killer, Brie would have said.

Trouble, Kat would have warned, while sizing him up from head to toe. And all areas in between.

"Elizabeth?"

She started. "Yes?"

He gave her a quizzical look. "I wonder where you go when you drift off like that."

"No place interesting." She shrugged. "Shall we?"

They took the elevator to the lower level where the laboratories were located. The basement was well-lit with several small labs radiating from the main hallway. At the end of the corridor was the largest facility, over ten-thousand square feet of space, implemented with millions of dollars of equipment including Olympus microscopes, Dell Optiplex microcomputers, a Cray C90 supercomputer and a Sorvall MicroUltra centrifuge. Thanks to the Pierces' passion for science, no expense had been spared.

Through the frosted-glass door that opened from the hallway, Elizabeth could see that the lights were on, and she assumed someone was working, a graduate student monitoring an experiment perhaps.

She opened the door and glanced inside. Paul Fortier, wearing a white lab coat, stood with his back to her, busy with something on one of the worktables.

"Dr. Fortier?"

Obviously he hadn't heard them come in because he spun, startled, and a test tube he held in one hand dropped to the pristine floor and smashed.

Red liquid splattered against the white tile.

Chapter Eight

"I'm sorry," Elizabeth said. "I didn't mean to startle you."

After his initial stunned reaction, Fortier managed to get his emotions under control—except for a slight muscle twitch in the side of his jaw. "Dr. Douglas! Don't you believe in knocking?"

"The door was unlocked," Elizabeth explained. "And I've never had to knock before entering the lab."

"Yes, well, it's not a good idea to sneak up on someone."

Not a good idea to hit on your students, either, Elizabeth thought. She'd heard via the rumor mill that some of them actually reciprocated his advances, but for the life of her, she couldn't understand the attraction. At best, Fortier was an average-looking man, around forty or so, with dark hair frosted at the temples and a neatly clipped beard and mustache. His eyes were a grayish green and closely set. His only outstanding feature was a rather prominent nose, which gave him a hawkish look, as if he were constantly on the lookout for prey.

Elizabeth took a step toward him. "I'll help you clean up—"

"No! No." He looked vaguely alarmed by her offer and quickly turned back to the worktable. "Just leave it. I'll attend to it myself." He picked up a plastic holder which contained several more glass vials, all filled with a red substance, and then walked over to store them in a nearby refrigerator.

The sight of the test tubes reminded Elizabeth of the one she and Cullen had found in the cooler room at the mortuary last night. And thinking about it brought back the same question. Who had left it there? In spite of what Cullen had said, Elizabeth knew there was no good reason for anyone on the staff to have a test tube in the cooler room. Fluid extractions and injections would be handled in the embalming room.

But if not someone who worked there, then who had brought the test tube into the cooler room? The killer? That didn't make much sense, either. If he'd wanted a sample of Bethany's blood or other bodily fluids, why not get it at the time of her murder? Judging by the condition of her body, he'd kept her for several days.

Elizabeth's gaze went to the broken test tube on the floor, then back to Fortier. She had no idea what kind of experiments he conducted in the lab. He'd always been very secretive about his work. Secretive about everything really.

The only thing Elizabeth knew about his private life—aside from the occasional dalliance with a student—was that he'd once been associated with a large lab in Boston specializing in gene therapy. Elizabeth's parents knew him slightly, and they'd hinted once that he'd given up research for teaching because he hadn't been able to cut it in the real world. Why else would one choose to teach? their disdainful tones had implied.

Fortier caught her staring at him and frowned. "Was there something you wanted, Dr. Douglas?"

"I'd like you to meet Professor Lucian LeCroix. He's the new chairman of the English Department. This is Dr. Fortier, chairman of our Biology Department."

"You'll excuse me if I don't shake hands." Fortier held up his hands, encased in thick latex gloves.

When Lucian didn't respond, Elizabeth glanced at him. He was staring at the red stain on the floor. He seemed almost mesmerized. "Is that blood?" he finally managed to ask.

"Animal blood," Fortier assured him. "But the lab rat was unharmed, so no cause for alarm."

Unharmed? Elizabeth glanced at the spill on the floor. No lab rat had given up that much blood and lived to tell the tale. She started to ask him the nature of his experiment, but thought better of it. Fortier was not only secretive about his work, but he could be resentful. Vindictive even. If he thought Elizabeth was prying into his business, he might get downright nasty.

"Elizabeth." Lucian's voice sounded urgent. He put a hand on her arm.

"Are you okay?" she asked quickly.

His hand crept from her arm to his throat, where he seemed on the verge of tearing open his collar. "Would you mind...if I waited for you outside? I think I need some air."

"Of course, but—"

He turned and hurried from the room before she could finish her thought. Fortier gave a low chuckle. "The new professor seems a little squeamish at the sight of blood."

"Luckily, he won't need to come into contact with it in the English Department," Elizabeth said dryly.

"Oh, I don't know. Some of today's literature is quite violent. Don't you keep up with your reading, Dr. Douglas?"

She shrugged. "I'm not much into fiction." Which wasn't at all true. She had a passion for certain kinds of fiction. She thought briefly about the prized volumes she kept under lock and key in her bedroom. "Don't you want some help with that?" She indicated the mess on the floor. "I feel somewhat responsible."

"I'll take care of it. Was there something else you needed?" He seemed anxious for her to leave.

Elizabeth hesitated. "You weren't at the Pierces' masquerade ball last night, were you?"

He gave a bitter laugh. "My invitation must have gotten lost in the mail. Why do you ask? Did anything noteworthy happen?"

Her gaze again strayed to the stain. There'd been no blood at all on Bethany's body. Nor on the floor beneath where she'd been hanged. No visible marks on the body...

It's almost as if the killer went out of his way to... preserve her, she'd told Cullen. The thought of that was almost as horrifying as mutilation.

Elizabeth glanced up. "As matter of fact, something did happen. A young woman was found dead. The police suspect foul play. It was Bethany Peters."

Fortier's gaze seemed to freeze for a moment, then

he turned quickly back to the counter, busying himself with a notepad and pen he kept handy. But Elizabeth didn't think he was taking notes. He acted like a man who was buying himself some time. "Bethany Peters?" he finally asked in a voice that sounded determinedly calm. "My God, what happened? Did they find who did it?"

"No, not yet."

"How did she die?"

With his back to her again, Elizabeth noticed several reddish brown smudges near the right elbow of his lab coat. The sleeve was ripped as well.

"The police don't know yet," she told him, her gaze on the rent. Had someone grabbed him and torn his coat? Someone with bloody fingers? "They're waiting for the autopsy."

Fortier turned then and his gaze met hers. Something about the way he looked at her—his eyes guarded, his expression absent of emotion—caused Elizabeth to shudder. One of his students had been found murdered last night, and he seemed at best mildly interested. "How do they know she was murdered?"

"She was hanged from a steel beam in the solarium at the Pierce estate."

"*Hanged?* Then I would think cause of death would be obvious."

"The police think she was dead before she was hanged. They believe she was killed elsewhere and brought to the Pierce mansion."

One dark brow lifted. "Why would someone go to that much trouble?"

A strangely detached way of putting it, surely. "I

don't know." Elizabeth hesitated again. "Bethany was a student of yours, wasn't she?"

His gaze turned icy, narrowed. "I hope you're not implying—"

"I'm not implying anything. I just wondered if she'd been absent from class the last few days."

He shrugged. "Come to think of it, she did miss a couple of classes last week. I just assumed she had the flu. It's going around campus. You had the bug yourself a few weeks ago as I recall."

True enough. She'd been sick that day when she'd bumped into him after a faculty meeting and thought he'd made a pass at her. Elizabeth had been in a feverish haze that day, not to mention highly medicated, and it was possible she'd dreamed the whole encounter. But in light of what had happened to Bethany, the exchange, real or imagined, took on an even more macabre sentiment.

She glanced up to find him watching her with that same odd speculation he'd had that day after the faculty meeting.

"The police may be around to talk to you," she said quickly, trying to dispel her sudden unease.

"The police?" He frowned. "Why would they want to talk to me?"

"They'll want to interview anyone who may have seen Bethany in the last day or so before she died. They'll want to know who her friends were, if she had a boyfriend, things like that."

Fortier's scowl deepened. "How would I know about any of that? She was just my student. A mediocre one at that." He struggled with his latex gloves for a moment, then tossed them to the counter. "What's your interest in all this anyway?"

"Bethany was a student here. Why wouldn't I be interested?"

He studied her for a moment. "You sound more than just interested. If I didn't know better, I'd swear you're trying to interrogate me, Dr. Douglas."

"Not at all." Elizabeth's heart started to pound. She knew it was time to leave, but she hadn't gotten all the answers she wanted. "I'm just asking you a few questions, preparing you for what the police are going to want to know."

"How good of you."

"So...you don't know anything about Bethany's social life?" she persisted.

"I don't keep tabs on my students any more than you do, Dr. Douglas. Although..."

"Yes?"

His expression turned coy. "I seem to recall a rumor going about a few weeks ago that Bethany had been seduced into a cult."

"A cult?" Elizabeth repeated in surprise. "What kind of cult?"

"I have no idea. I don't even know if it's true. You know how students talk. You hear things that more or less go in one ear and out the other. I never put much credence in rumors."

Elizabeth somehow doubted that was true. She had a feeling Fortier paid very close attention to the latest talk on campus because, more often than not, the juiciest morsels involved him.

She turned toward the door, then paused. "By the way, Dr. Fortier, you seem to have torn your lab coat."

He grabbed his right elbow, although Elizabeth had made no mention of where the coat was ripped. "Ah, yes. I snagged it on a nail earlier. I'd forgotten all about it.''

"Did you cut yourself as well? That looks like blood on the fabric.''

He looked faintly surprised. Then almost amused. "Blood? It may well be. You know how experiments can get a bit...messy at times.'' He turned back to the counter, away from Elizabeth's probing gaze. "Good day, Dr. Douglas.''

"Good day,'' Elizabeth responded, glancing once again at the blood that had been spilled on the floor.

LUCIAN GAVE HER a sheepish smile when she came out of the building. "Sorry for running out on you like that. I, uh, just needed to get some fresh air.''

Why couldn't he just admit the sight of blood made him ill?

Elizabeth thought back to the previous night, to Cullen's discomfort in the solarium. He obviously suffered from claustrophobia, but for some reason, he couldn't bring himself to acknowledge it. Why couldn't men just own up to their weaknesses? Why try to hide them? Didn't they know such peccadilloes often endeared them to women?

"Are you okay?''

His grin widened, displaying teeth that were dazzlingly white in the sunshine. "I'm fine. Never felt better. Shall we head back?'' They started walking toward the library, keeping a brisk pace against the cold. "How well do you know Fortier?''

Elizabeth adjusted the stocking cap over her ears. It had been warm in the lab, but she was glad to be back outside, even in the freezing wind. Paul Fortier had that effect on her. "He's been here for several years, but I can't say I know him all that well. Why?"

Lucian's expression turned pensive. "He struck me as an odd sort, that's all."

"He is a little on the strange side," Elizabeth agreed. "I'm sure you'll hear the stories about him soon enough."

"What kind of stories?"

She hesitated. "I really shouldn't spread rumors about my colleagues. I wouldn't want them talking about me behind my back."

"Yet you did bring it up," Lucian pointed out. "You must think it's something I need to know."

"Heathrow is an all-girl school as you well know, and there aren't that many eligible young men in Moriah's Landing. Sometimes hormones…"

"Run amok?" he supplied.

Elizabeth blushed, thinking about her own rampaging hormones the night before with Cullen. "There've been rumors about Dr. Fortier and some of his students."

"Are you saying he's had affairs with students?"

"Maybe. There was an incident a few years back that almost got him fired. A student claimed he'd assaulted her. She later recanted, admitting that she'd wanted revenge for a failing grade. Dr. Fortier was completely exonerated, and the student transferred to another school. The talk died down after a while, but it never went away completely. I've always wondered…"

"You've always wondered if he really did assault that young woman and then somehow bought her off."

Elizabeth drew a long, cold breath. "I really don't think I should say any more about it."

"I understand." They walked along in silence for a moment, then Lucian said unexpectedly, "What kind of experiment do you think he was working on?"

"His field is molecular biology, and I know he has a lot of training in genetics. He used to work for the Massachusetts Institute for Human Gene Therapy."

"Interesting," Lucian mused. "What brought him to Moriah's Landing, do you suppose?"

Elizabeth gave him a sidelong glance. "I don't know, but I could ask you the same thing." She paused. "Your resumé is quite impressive, I understand. You were tenured at a very prestigious university. You could have gone anywhere, Professor LeCroix. Why Heathrow?"

"It's Lucian, remember? I thought we agreed."

"Lucian, then."

She waited for him to reply to her original question. He took a moment to consider it. "I needed to get away."

She glanced at him in surprise. "From what?"

"Boston." He lifted a shoulder. "Without going into a long, sordid explanation, let's just say the offer from Dr. Barloft came at an opportune time."

"I...see." But, of course, she didn't. His answer was vague at best.

As if sensing her curiosity, he shrugged again. "I was in a relationship. It ended badly."

"Oh."

He gave her an amused glance. "To put it bluntly, I was involved with a married woman. I gave her an ultimatum, and she decided to stay with her husband. A graceful exit was all that was left to me.''

''I'm sorry,'' Elizabeth said. ''I didn't mean to pry.''

''So now you know why I came to Heathrow.'' He stopped and when she gazed up at him, he said softly, ''I can't help wondering why you've stayed.''

''At Heathrow? I told you. It's the first place I ever truly felt at home.''

His gaze on her deepened. ''You had an unhappy childhood?''

She hesitated, not certain how much she wanted to reveal about herself to a stranger. ''I had a lonely childhood.''

''You were an only child?''

''Until four years ago. Now I have an adorable little brother.''

He seemed intrigued by the notion. ''Why did your parents wait so long to have another child?''

''I've wondered that myself,'' Elizabeth admitted. ''I think it was because—'' *They'd given up on me,* she almost blurted. ''They were both approaching middle age. Maybe they had some sort of crisis. Instead of buying sports cars or having affairs, they decided to have a baby.''

As he stared down at her, something flashed in his eyes. A look of regret. Was he thinking about the woman he'd left behind in Boston? Was he wondering if he'd done the right thing?

''I'm not sure how we got off on this topic,'' Elizabeth murmured. She turned and resumed walking toward the library.

''Neither am I. You were telling me about Dr. Fortier. He used to work in genetics—'' Lucian broke off, and Elizabeth glanced up at him. He was gazing straight ahead, his expression wary.

She turned then, following his gaze, and her heart almost leaped from her chest. Cullen was at the bottom of the library steps, pacing back and forth in the cold. He had on his long, black overcoat, not elegantly fitted as Lucian's was, but loose and flowing, hem flapping in the wind. He didn't wear a hat, but he wasn't impervious to the weather. His complexion was ruddy with cold, and his hands were shoved deeply into his pockets.

When he spotted Elizabeth and Lucian, he stopped pacing and strode toward them. ''Elizabeth.'' He gave her a curt nod.

''Cullen.'' What was he doing here? How had he known where to find her? Or was she being presumptuous? Maybe his being here was just coincidence, and he wasn't even looking for her.

But his expectant expression told her that he was. Elizabeth remembered in Technicolor detail the way he'd looked at her last night, his obvious fascination with the low cut of her gown. Then he'd fled her house in great haste because…why? He'd realized suddenly that she was a woman? That he might be attracted to her?

That he wanted her?

A thrill of adrenaline shot through Elizabeth's veins. It was a heady experience, the possibility of having a man—two men, she amended, glancing at Lucian—interested in her.

But at the moment, neither of them was paying her the slightest bit of attention. They were too busy sizing one another up. And by the look on Cullen's face, he wasn't all that impressed with Lucian. The latter was harder to read.

Elizabeth said quickly, "Cullen, I'd like you to meet Professor Lucian LeCroix. Lucian, this is Detective Ryan—"

"We've met," Cullen said, not happily.

"Last night," Lucian explained. "Detective Ryan spoke with most of the guests, I believe."

For the first time in her life, Elizabeth felt completely at a loss for words. There was no reason in the world for the encounter to be so awkward, and yet it was. She even felt a little guilty, and she couldn't for the life of her figure out why.

But Cullen was obviously displeased with her about something. He frowned down at her. "Do you have a minute?"

"I was just showing Lucian around campus—"

"It's quite all right," Lucian said graciously. He turned to Elizabeth and took her hand. "I've taken up enough of your time, but I enjoyed the morning immensely."

"So did I. I hope you'll be happy here at Heathrow."

"Oh, I think the chances of that are quite excellent," he said with a knowing smile. He brought her gloved hand up to his lips. "Till next time, Elizabeth."

Once he'd walked away, Cullen turned with a smirk. "That's laying it on thick. Who does that clown think he is anyway?"

"Shush! He'll hear you," Elizabeth snapped.

Cullen's brows soared. "Since when does Lizzie Douglas worry about what anyone thinks?" He reached out and yanked on her stocking cap.

"Don't call me that. I detest that name." Elizabeth batted his hand away, annoyed that he seemed intent on returning their relationship to the teasing one they'd had in high school. Those days were long gone. She wasn't a little kid anymore, and Cullen damn well knew it.

And that, Elizabeth thought, was the problem. At least for him.

She gave him a challenging glance. "So what are you doing here?"

He couldn't quite meet her gaze. "I came looking for you."

"And how did you know where to find me?"

He shrugged. "Someone mentioned you were meeting LeCroix here at the library this morning."

"Who told you that?"

He glanced at her then, his expression slightly reproachful. "I never reveal my sources, Elizabeth."

"You don't have to. I know who it was." No one but Becca Smith knew about her meeting with Lucian, but why would Becca tell Cullen? Why would the subject even come up...unless they'd been discussing Elizabeth in the first place?

Don't read too much into that, either, she warned herself. The conversation had probably been in reference to Bethany's murder. Hadn't Lucian said that Cullen had talked to everyone at the ball?

Still, it gave Elizabeth a strange feeling to think of Cullen talking about her—in any regard—with her friends.

"Why were you looking for me?" she tried to ask nonchalantly.

"I came to ask for your help."

Elizabeth gaped at him in astonishment. "My help? With what?"

"The case."

"The case—" Surprise turned to suspicion. Elizabeth narrowed her eyes as she studied him. This had to be a trick. The Cullen Ryan she knew would never have made such an about-face over the course of a few hours. Not unless something—or someone—had persuaded him to. "Was this your idea or Chief Redfern's?"

"Redfern's?" His brow furrowed. "Why would you think that?"

Elizabeth lifted her gloved hands and blew on them for warmth. "Because you made it clear last night you didn't want my help. Why the change of heart?"

"Does it matter?" He stared out over the campus, his tone and demeanor impatient. "Why do you have to make this so damned difficult?"

"What?"

"Apologizing to you."

Elizabeth's mouth dropped again. "Is *that* what you're doing?"

"Apparently not too well." He hunched his shoulders against the cold as he turned to face her. His eyes glistened in the sunlight like twin glaciers, cool, hard, invincible. For the first time, Elizabeth noticed a tiny white scar that clipped his left eyebrow, and she wondered what had happened to him. Had he always had the scar? She didn't think so. She would have remembered.

There was very little about Cullen Ryan that she'd forgotten. Except, perhaps, for the extraordinary hold he seemed to have on her.

Earlier, when she'd sensed Lucian's attraction, the

knowledge had made her feel empowered. But with Cullen...with Cullen she never knew quite what to say or how to act. She never knew what he expected of her.

"Maybe I should try this again," he said in a more conciliatory tone. "I was wrong, okay? About shutting you out of the investigation, I mean. Not about the contamination of the crime scene," he was quick to add. "Or about tampering with evidence. I meant what I said about that stunt you pulled last night. You shouldn't have gone to the funeral home without my permission. That little visit could still come back to haunt us. You should have known better."

This was an apology? "All that groveling, Cullen. It really isn't becoming."

He cut her a wry glance. "Maybe I should just get to the point."

"I think that's probably best," she agreed.

"The police department here in town has very limited resources. I'm the only detective in the Criminal Investigations Unit, and I was promoted mainly because none of the other cops wanted the extra paperwork. It had nothing to do with my ability, but just for the record, I'm a damn good detective."

"I never doubted it."

He shrugged off her endorsement. "But the equipment we have at our disposal, the computer system—" He shook his head in disgust. "You wouldn't believe the antiquated stuff we have to put up with. Most of the officers on the force are good men, but their training, and frankly their experience, is limited. The state police lab in Sudbury is helping us out, and they'd probably be willing to send an investigator if we requested one. But I don't think Chief Redfern would agree to that. He's a stickler for jurisdiction. In other words—''

''I'm all you've got.''

He drew a long breath, gazing down at her. ''That's why I'm here. You have an advanced degree in criminology. That's more than anyone in the department has, including me.'' He paused. ''In spite of the impression I may have given you last night, I'm not about to let a killer go free because I'm too proud to ask for help.''

Elizabeth had a feeling it had taken a lot for him to admit that. ''What do you want me to do?''

''For starters,'' he said grimly, ''I think we'd better take another look at that body.''

''That's what—'' She'd been about to say that was what she'd wanted to do all along, but for once in her life, Elizabeth thought before she spoke. Swallowing her own pride, she muttered, ''That sounds like a good idea to me.''

Chapter Nine

"It looks like an incision." Elizabeth bent over the body, examining the tiny slit on Bethany's throat, the only visible mark they'd found so far. The body was still at the funeral home, awaiting transport to the county hospital for the autopsy. She glanced up. "You found this last night?"

"Dr. Vogel spotted it," Cullen told her.

"What did he make of it?"

"He said it looks like it may have been made to expose the carotid artery."

Elizabeth's heart jumped. She looked at Cullen, startled. Horrified. "You mean he bled her?"

"We won't know that until the autopsy."

Elizabeth returned her gaze to the body. "I can see what appears to be needle tracks on the inside of her left arm."

Cullen nodded. "I saw those, too. Hear any rumors on campus about her being into drugs?"

Elizabeth shook her head. She wore latex gloves, as did Cullen, and she reached out now to gently position Bethany's arm for a better look at the marks.

"Even if these are needle tracks, as we suspect, I doubt they were self-inflicted."

"I agree. They were carefully camouflaged, just like the incision, to avoid obvious detection. But why go to all that trouble, and then hang her?"

"The hanging is probably symbolic of something."

"What?"

"Witches?" Elizabeth shrugged. "I don't know. But I did hear today that she may have been involved with a cult."

Cullen's voice sharpened. "Who told you that?"

"Paul Fortier. Do you know him?" Elizabeth looked up, and when Cullen shook his head, she said, "He's head of the Biology Department at Heathrow. Bethany was in one of his classes."

Cullen lifted a brow. "And?"

"And he said he'd heard rumors that Bethany may have been seduced into a cult." Elizabeth straightened, gazing at Cullen over the metal tray that held Bethany's body. Cold air circulated into the room from the open cooler, and she shivered.

Cullen frowned. "You heard anything on campus about a cult?"

She shook her head. "Not a word."

He thought for a moment. "What do you know about Fortier? I get the feeling you're holding something back."

Elizabeth hesitated, reluctant to convey her feelings to Cullen. They were just feelings, after all, and it didn't seem right to plant seeds of doubt in his head because she didn't like Fortier. Because she found him creepy. She thought again about the tear in his lab coat, the stains that might have been blood.... *Experiments can get a bit messy at times.* "It's nothing concrete. He's just a bit strange, that's all. When I went by the lab today, he was working on an experiment. I startled him when I came in, and he dropped a test tube of blood. It made me think of the test tube we found in here last night."

"You think Fortier was here last night?"

"No, not really. It's just—"

"Go on."

She glanced down at Bethany's pale body. "I think it might be a good idea to talk to some of the girls who knew Bethany. Find out if she had a relationship with Fortier besides teacher/student."

"So that's it." Cullen's features hardened in disgust. "He's the kind of guy who hits on his students."

"I've heard rumors," Elizabeth admitted.

Cullen's gaze narrowed on her. "Has he hit on you?"

When Elizabeth hesitated again, Cullen muttered something under his breath.

"What?"

"Nothing. Just answer the question, Elizabeth. Has Fortier made a pass at you?"

"I wouldn't call it a pass, exactly," she evaded. "He said something to me the other day, and it's been bothering me."

"What did he say to you?" Something in Cullen's tone made Elizabeth glance up in surprise. "Tell me."

"It was when I was sick," she said. "I bumped

into him at a faculty meeting, and I knew I was still contagious. Plus, I looked just awful. You know how you get after a bout with the flu, like death warmed over. Anyway, I stepped back from him, and I think I said, 'Stay away. I'm dying.' I had a high fever, so I may have gotten things confused, but I remember him telling me that I'd never looked lovelier, which was ridiculous. Then he said something like, 'What is it they say? There's nothing quite so beautiful or poetic as a dead or dying woman.' I was too sick to think much about it at first, but now I can't seem to get it out of my head.'' She shuddered.

"Sounds like Poe."

"I beg your pardon?"

Cullen's expression was slightly challenging. "I think he's paraphrasing Edgar Allen Poe. 'The death of a beautiful woman is unquestionably the most poetic subject in the world.'" When Elizabeth continued to stare at him, he shrugged. "Don't look so surprised. I do know how to read."

"It's not that—" Although she couldn't deny he *had* taken her by surprise. Here was a side of Cullen she'd never seen before. Thoughtful, insightful. Intellectual. "I should have made the connection myself."

The corners of his mouth twitched, as if he were amused by her self-recrimination. "I guess even geniuses slip up once in a while."

"I slip up all the time," she said softly.

Their gazes met and clung again, and for a moment, Elizabeth forgot where they were. Forgot that a beautiful dead girl literally lay between them.

And that a murderer still went free.

With an effort, she tore her gaze from Cullen and glanced down at Bethany. Even in death, she was still very lovely.

"Poe had a fixation with beautiful dead women," she mused. "It was a constant theme in his writing. Think of some of his most famous poems. 'The Raven.' 'To Helen.' 'Annabel Lee.' You don't think—" Elizabeth stopped, reluctant to voice the horror going through her head.

"No," Cullen said grimly. "I don't. Not yet at least. But without any other viable suspects, I'd say Fortier bears closer scrutiny, especially if it turns out he really was having a relationship with the deceased."

"Poor Bethany," Elizabeth murmured. Had she been the obsession of a madman, or had she simply been caught at the wrong place at the wrong time?

"There's something about all this that's bothering me," Cullen said. "If the killer knows his victim, if his rage is something personal, he'll go for the face. We don't have that here." He waved a gloved hand toward the body. "No sign of a sexual assault, either." He shook his head. "It's like you said. It looks as if he went out of his way to preserve her."

"It's time."

They both whirled as a whispery voice spoke from behind them. Ned Krauter had entered the cooler room so quietly neither of them had heard him. He stood just inside the door, primly dressed in a somber black suit and starched shirt, the only adornment a single white carnation fastened to his lapel.

He was a small man, not much taller than Elizabeth, but wiry. His hands were clasped beneath his chin, as if in deep prayer or meditation, and Elizabeth couldn't help noticing that his fingers were very long and tapered, almost feminine-looking.

She imagined those hands administering to the dead, carefully applying rouge and lip gloss to create a more lifelike appearance. And her thoughts reminded her of the close encounter with the undertaker the night before, how he'd come into the viewing room to speak to Mrs. Presco's corpse.

Perhaps Paul Fortier wasn't the only one who found poetry in death.

Slowly, Mr. Krauter walked across the room to join them at the cooler. He gazed down at the body, his pale countenance almost rapt. "So young," he said tragically. "So beautiful." He reached out a hand, as if to stroke her cheek, but instead he merely clung to the tray for a moment, caressing the cold metal with his thumb. "It's time," he repeated, his tone so hushed and deferential he appeared to be speaking to no one but Bethany.

"Time for what?" Cullen asked.

"What?" Krauter glanced up, his eyes unfocused for a moment. "Oh, the…autopsy. The ambulance from the county hospital is here." He returned his gaze to the body, his expression softening. "But not to worry," he whispered. "It will all be over soon."

THAT NIGHT Cullen went by the Beachway Diner to have a bite to eat before heading back to the station to put in a few more hours on the case. He'd already been working nearly twenty-four hours straight, but he still had witness interviews he needed to go over, and he wanted to have another look at the evidence log, meager as it was.

As it had been the previous evening, the diner was almost deserted, but Cullen suspected news of the murder had kept would-be customers indoors tonight. He took a booth in the corner and noticed that the two patrons besides himself were the same as last night, as well. Shamus McManus and Marley Glasglow. They were seated at the bar, several stools apart, each appearing lost in his own thoughts.

Cullen was glad he'd chosen a booth. He didn't feel much like conversation tonight, especially when he knew what the subject would be.

Brie was on duty again, and when she came to take his order, Cullen thought she looked tired. The sparkle in her green eyes—the first thing he usually noticed about her—was missing.

When she came back with his clam chowder a few minutes later, he said sympathetically, "Don't they ever give you time off from this place?"

She shrugged. "I've been working some odd hours now that I'm back in school, and I have to accommodate my class schedule."

"That doesn't give you much time for a social life," he commented.

"Nicole is my social life. Any spare time I have I spend with her."

When he gave her a blank stare, she smiled and like magic, the sparkle popped back into her eyes. "My daughter. The most beautiful three-year-old you ever saw."

"I can believe that," Cullen said, paying her a subtle compliment.

She blushed with pleasure. "You're a nice man, Cullen." Then added playfully, "I don't care what anyone says."

"Thanks." It was strange to think of someone younger than he already having a kid. Cullen couldn't imagine himself as a father, maybe because he didn't want to. Maybe because he was afraid he'd see himself being the kind of parent his old man had been.

"You've been putting in some long hours yourself, haven't you?" Brie asked sympathetically.

"Yeah."

"That murder." She shook her head. "What a terrible thing."

"It's bad," he agreed.

"I heard Elizabeth Douglas found the body at the Pierce mansion."

Cullen stared up at her curiously, watching the play of emotions across her features. "You and Elizabeth are friends, aren't you?"

"We used to be. We kind of lost touch after I dropped out of school." She smiled sadly. "We all get caught up in our own lives, I guess. You know how it is."

He nodded. "So what are the local gossips making of the murder?"

Brie glanced over her shoulder, then lowered her voice. "They're saying McFarland Leary rose from his grave last night and killed that poor girl. He hanged her just like they hanged him. They say he killed all those women twenty years ago, too, including Kat Ridgemont's mother.''

''That may be what some are saying,'' Cullen said grimly. ''The other half is certain David Bryson is the killer. We've even heard rumblings of a vigilante group forming.'' He could picture it now. A mob of outraged citizens traipsing up Old Mountain Road with torches and ropes, maybe a few crosses thrown in for good measure. A scene straight from a horror flick. Just what they needed.

Brie leaned slightly toward him. ''I don't think the killer is Leary or David Bryson.''

Cullen lifted a brow. ''You have a theory?''

She angled her head ever so slightly toward the counter, where Marley Glasglow sat hunched over his coffee. ''If I were you, I'd find out where he went after he left here last night.''

Actually, Cullen had already checked, and, as it turned out, Glasglow didn't have an alibi. But there wasn't any physical evidence or eyewitness accounts tying him to the murder, either. Not yet, at least.

Cullen thought about Elizabeth's ''flash of yellow'' on the terrace outside the solarium, and he remembered that Glasglow had been wearing a yellow rain slicker last night. So had Shamus McManus for that matter, but for the life of him, Cullen couldn't picture that old geezer a killer.

Although…Shamus had made some rather strange claims. What the hell had he been rambling on about? Something about Leary rising from his grave to look for his offspring and the offspring of their offspring?

Was it possible Shamus knew something, perhaps inadvertently, about the murder?

Now you're grasping at straws, Cullen warned himself. *That's what exhaustion and lack of any real leads will do for you.*

He doubted Shamus could be of much help, and as strongly as Cullen believed Glasglow capable of such a heinous crime, the man wasn't going to be convicted because he owned a yellow rain slicker. If that were the case, three-quarters of the town would end up behind bars.

But even as that thought entered his head, Glasglow slowly swiveled on his stool until he was facing Cullen. And for just a moment, for that one split second when their gazes met, Cullen could have sworn he was staring into the eyes of a killer.

Chapter Ten

On Monday afternoon, Cullen found himself once again at Heathrow College, looking for Elizabeth. It was becoming a habit, and probably not a very smart one. She wasn't at all the type of woman he needed to get involved with. For one thing, he still had a hard time thinking of her as a woman. At twenty, she wasn't much more than a kid.

She's only four years younger than you.

And she has a body that won't quit.

Okay, granted she wasn't that much younger than he was, and granted she'd done a lot of maturing since he'd left town six years ago. The way she'd looked in that sexy costume the other night had been evidence of that. The low-cut neckline had revealed plenty of her...maturity. Cullen's testosterone levels had shot through the roof when he'd seen her. He hadn't felt an attraction that intense in a long time.

But the problem was, he also still had images of the way she'd been in high school, a brainy, snooty little geek whose air of superiority had rubbed people the wrong way. To be fair, her attitude had probably been a defense against the way the older kids picked on her, but she'd still been as annoying as hell back then.

Even so, Cullen had always found himself coming to her rescue, which, come to think of it, really hadn't been that much of a hardship, considering how he'd liked a good fight. But there'd been something about her even then that had touched a chord inside him, that had made him want to defend her. Made him want to be her hero.

Which was stupid. The two of them couldn't have been more unalike. They came from two very different worlds. But even more of a chasm than their social status was Elizabeth's intelligence. She was a Ph.D. at the age of twenty; he'd quit school his senior year and hitchhiked out of town. He'd later earned his diploma and had distinguished himself at the police academy. But the stigma of being a dropout still clung to him, especially in Moriah's Landing.

All his life, Cullen had been ashamed of something—his mother running off the way she had, his father's drinking, Cullen's own weaknesses and temptations. He'd gotten into a lot of trouble as a kid because of those temptations. He'd hung out with thugs until he'd become one himself, and he still wore that stigma, too. He was a product of his parents, but that was no excuse. There was a time when he'd been no better than they.

Being a cop was the first thing in his life he'd ever had to be proud of. What if he lost that?

Are you afraid to let me see the body, Cullen?

Why would I be afraid?

Maybe you think I'll find something you didn't.

He drew a breath, remembering his conversation with Elizabeth. What if she *had* seen something on the body that he hadn't? What if she could solve this case when he couldn't? What if she were to take away the only thing in his life he'd ever been any good at?

And that, he knew, was one of the reasons for his initial reluctance about using her on this case.

But he wasn't proud of the way he'd acted with her. He didn't want to be like some of the cops he'd known in Boston—or like Chief Redfern, for that matter—who were willing to jeopardize investigations because of their petty squabbles and insufferable egos. A young woman was dead, and the killer was still out there somewhere. Cullen would do whatever it took to stop that maniac before he could kill again, and if his own pride got stepped on in the process, then so be it.

He located the classroom where Elizabeth was conducting a lecture, and he slipped in quietly so as not to create a stir. Only a few students seated at the back turned to stare at him, and they probably hadn't been paying attention in the first place, he decided.

Elizabeth stood at the front of the classroom, her back to him as she scribbled something on the blackboard. She continued to talk as she wrote. "...relationship between mental illness and criminality, and the implications that psychiatric labeling of deviant behavior has on the criminal offender, both in and out of the courts—"

She turned then and saw him. Her expression froze. Her body went rigid for just a moment as their gazes clung, and something electric leaped between them.

Then she regained her composure and nodded briefly before continuing her lecture. She was in her element in the classroom. She seemed small, but perfectly capable. Utterly fearless, and Cullen wondered suddenly why he'd ever felt the need to come to her defense.

He tried to concentrate on what she was saying. Evidently the topic was abnormal behavior and criminality, but he found his mind and his gaze wandering. He couldn't stop looking at her. He couldn't stop thinking about the other night at her cottage when she'd bent to pour the tea, how her breasts—firm and small and incredibly tempting—had been exposed by the cut of her gown. Before that night, he'd never seen Elizabeth wear anything remotely revealing. He'd never considered her as anything but mildly attractive. Certainly not sexy. Certainly not ravishing.

But that costume had inspired all kinds of fantasies. If he'd gone to bed that night, Cullen was sure he would have dreamed about that dress. About slowly sliding it down her body, until more than just a tantalizing bit of cleavage was exposed....

The room was warm, and he realized suddenly that he was sweating beneath his coat.

When class was finally dismissed, the students pushed past him on their way to the hall. Some of them bumped up against him on purpose while their friends giggled and encouraged them. One slipped a note in his hand, and he glanced down to see a phone number and a smiley face sketched on pink paper. When he looked back up, a shapely blonde winked at him from the doorway.

Heathrow, with its all-girl student body, was a frat boy's wildest dream come true. But even though the girls weren't that much younger than Cullen, certainly not jailbait, he wasn't the least bit interested in any of them. He told himself it was because he had too much on his mind, but when he glanced up and saw

Elizabeth waiting for him at the front of the classroom, he realized with a sinking sensation why none of the young women appealed to him.

They weren't Elizabeth.

You can't let this happen, a little voice warned him as he approached her warily.

What did he have to offer a woman like her?

"Hello." Her smile was tentative, shy. Very appealing.

Too bad she didn't still wear braces, Cullen thought. Too bad she wasn't still scrawny and annoying. Well, she could still be annoying. But she sure as hell wasn't scrawny, he noted, his gaze traveling over her.

She was dressed in gray wool slacks and a matching sweater that were not at all suggestive, and yet Cullen couldn't help noticing the way the fabric clung to her gentle curves. The way her hair, pulled back in a bun, highlighted her smooth complexion. The way her hazel eyes glinted with intelligence.

"What are you doing here?" she asked.

He cleared his throat. "I came by to see Fortier."

Her brows lifted. "Did you talk to him? What did you find out? What did he tell you?"

Cullen held up a hand. "Whoa. Slow down. No need to get so excited." He saw her blush a little and thought how unusual in this day and age to see a woman so easily embarrassed. How different she was from the women he'd dated in Boston. She wore no makeup, but there was a natural glow to her complexion. A natural sparkle in her eyes even under such sobering conditions.

"Fortier didn't add anything that you hadn't already told me," he said. "He even sort of backtracked on the cult thing. Said he couldn't swear it had been Bethany he'd heard some of the girls talking about.''

"Do you believe him?"

Cullen shrugged. "He's hard to read. I'd swear he's hiding something, but a lot of people get nervous and evasive when they talk to a cop." He paused. "I actually stopped by for another reason. The preliminary autopsy report is in. I thought you might be interested in the results. We were right about that incision. Cause of death was exsanguination. The body was severely drained of blood."

Elizabeth shuddered. "What about the needle marks on her arm?"

"The toxicology screen was clean, so it's not likely she was shooting up. Nor was she injected involuntarily." Cullen paused, not anxious to get into the more grisly aspects of the report. "According to the medical examiner, the incision was made on the superior border of the sternoclavicular notch, exposing the carotid artery. He thinks a large needle may have been inserted into the artery and was probably joined to a length of tubing connected to a pump. Evidently, it's a procedure very common in embalming, where fluid is pumped in and the blood is flushed out. The whole procedure wouldn't have taken long. While she remained alive, the victim's heart would have helped speed the process."

Cullen saw the horror dawn in Elizabeth's eyes, and he wished suddenly that he hadn't brought her this news. He needed her help, but it didn't seem right dragging her into something this gruesome.

"My God, Cullen," she said in a hushed tone. "Why would someone take that much blood from her? And what about the needle marks? Did he try to draw blood from her veins first? Did he try to keep her alive while he—'' She broke off, her eyes closing briefly. ''What are we dealing with here?''

''A killer,'' he said. ''A pretty damn sick one.''

But Elizabeth had already turned away from him and was pacing back and forth in front of the blackboard. She stopped suddenly and glanced up. ''What about Ned Krauter? He would know about this procedure.''

''So would every other undertaker in the county. And every doctor, for that matter. Any hospital or laboratory, as well as funeral homes, would probably have the necessary equipment.''

Elizabeth nodded. ''You're right. They'd also have the facilities to dispose of the evidence. Still, it is a medical procedure. That could narrow the field.'' She paused. ''I keep thinking about those murders twenty years ago. Do you remember much about them?''

Cullen shrugged. ''Not really. I was just a kid at the time.''

''I wasn't even born when the first killing took place,'' Elizabeth said. ''It was Kat Ridgemont's mother. At least, it was assumed she was the first victim. But cause of death was always a bit sketchy. The police refused to release certain details to the public for obvious reasons, one undoubtedly being they were afraid of a copycat killer.'' She glanced up at Cullen. ''Something tells me you need to get a look at those old case files. Do you think they're still around?''

''In the archives, probably. Or in the cold-case file. Let's go take a look.''

"Really?" She sounded surprised. "You want me to come with you?"

"It was your idea."

"I know, but..." She hesitated, looking suddenly very young and unsure of herself. "I keep thinking you'll change your mind. You won't want my help."

He gazed down at her, feeling emotions he had no business feeling. "I came here today, didn't I?"

She swallowed. "Yes, I guess you did at that. Does Chief Redfern know you're consulting with me on this case?"

Cullen's expression hardened. "I don't really give a damn what he knows. I'm not about to let what happened here twenty years ago happen again."

"Even if it means you have to collaborate with me?" she asked him shyly.

"Even if it means I have to collaborate with the devil himself."

"Let's hope it doesn't come to that," she said in a completely serious voice.

ELIZABETH STUDIED Cullen's profile as they drove toward the police station. She still couldn't believe he'd changed his mind about using her in the investigation, but she understood his reasoning. He was willing to do whatever was necessary to solve this case, even consult with her.

But a secret part of Elizabeth still held out hope that it was more than just her expertise he sought. She wanted to believe that he trusted her. Respected her. That he might even be looking for a reason to spend more time with her.

Then again, maybe he wasn't, she thought as she contemplated his grim expression. Maybe all that was on his mind was finding a killer, and that's what she should be concentrating on, too.

He turned suddenly, catching her gaze, and her heart tilted inside her. There it was again, that flutter of awareness, that tingly thrill that coursed through her body every time Cullen looked her way. Every time he came near her. If this was a schoolgirl crush, she showed no signs of outgrowing it.

His gray eyes, brooding and sexy, watched her for a moment before he turned his gaze back to the road. "When did Fortier first come to Heathrow?"

"A few years ago."

"Can you be more specific?"

"Well, let's see." Elizabeth thought for a moment. "He came at the beginning of my first full-time semester, so it must have been five years ago."

Cullen glanced at her. "Just before Claire Cavendish was abducted."

"Yes, as a matter of fact."

"Do you happen to know if she was in any of his classes?"

"I'm pretty sure she was. I remember the girls talking about him. Kat, Brie, Tasha and Claire. They were all freshmen that year, and technically I was, too. It was my first year on campus, but I already had enough credits to take senior-level classes, so I didn't have Fortier. I was only fifteen at the time, and pretty naive. I may have misconstrued some of the innuendo, but I think he may have hit on one of them."

"Claire?"

"I don't know. I suppose I could ask Brie and Kat if they remember." Although she rarely spoke to her old friends these days. Not that they'd had a falling out or anything. They'd all just drifted apart. She'd heard Brie had started back at school, but Elizabeth never saw her.

"What about Professor LeCroix?"

Was it her imagination, or had Cullen's tone changed slightly? She gave him a sidelong glance. "What about Lucian?"

The corners of his mouth tightened. "It's Lucian, is it?"

"He *is* my colleague."

"So is Fortier, but I don't hear you call him by his first name."

Elizabeth shrugged. "I've never liked Dr. Fortier."

"But you do like LeCroix?"

"I don't know him well enough yet to make that determination, but he's interesting. And charming." And if Elizabeth didn't know better, she'd swear Cullen was displaying subtle signs of jealousy, but that was probably hoping for too much.

He glanced at her, his gaze cool and appraising. "Has it occurred to you yet that you discovered Bethany's body on the day Lucian LeCroix arrived in town?"

Elizabeth stared at him in surprise. "You're not suggesting he had something to do with her death, are you? Bethany died days earlier before I found her."

"We don't know for sure when she died. The M.E. was unable to make that determination."

"But…we have a pretty good idea, judging by the condition of the body. And besides, Lucian didn't even know her."

"That's a fairly broad assumption, Elizabeth. You can't know that, either."

"But you said yourself, he arrived in town on the day her body was found. If she died days earlier—"

"What makes you think they didn't know each other from somewhere else? Boston, maybe."

"Was Bethany from Boston?"

"As a matter of fact, she was."

Elizabeth folded her arms in an unconsciously defensive gesture. "But that doesn't mean they knew each other."

"It doesn't mean they didn't, either. Bethany was from a wealthy family, and so is LeCroix, from what I've been able to gather. Who's to say they didn't know each other? Who's to say they weren't involved?"

"I don't think they were," Elizabeth insisted.

Cullen gave her a frowning glance. "Why not?"

"Because he was involved with a married woman before he accepted the job at Heathrow. That's why he came here. He left a tenured position at a prestigious university because this woman, whoever she is, decided to stay with her husband."

"What a noble guy," Cullen muttered. "LeCroix told you all this?"

"Most of it. Some of it I heard through the faculty grapevine. Evidently, Lucian's mentor and Dr. Barloft, the president of Heathrow, are old childhood friends. That's how Lucian knew about the position here." She paused, her gaze on Cullen. "Why are you so suspicious of him? He hardly fits the profile of our killer."

"How do you know?"

"Because he doesn't have a medical background."

"How do you know he wasn't a premed student before he changed his major?"

She glanced at him sharply. "Do you know something about him I don't?"

"No," Cullen admitted. "There's just something about that guy..." He scowled at the road.

"What?"

"I don't know." He lifted his hand from the steering wheel to massage the back of his neck. "He's a little too smooth, if you ask me. A little too perfect."

"He's very handsome," Elizabeth commented, eyeing Cullen carefully.

"If you like that type."

"I imagine a lot of women do."

Cullen said something under his breath as he whipped the car into a parking space in front of the police station, something Elizabeth was quite certain she wasn't meant to hear.

He killed the engine and turned, his expression closed, his gaze shuttered. "Be careful with that guy, Elizabeth."

"What do you mean?"

"I've seen his type before. He's a real player. And a girl like you—"

She cut him off with an icy glare. "A girl like me, what?"

"You could get in over your head, that's all."

Anger washed over her, and she turned toward the door, reaching for the handle. "Thanks for the warning, but I can take care of myself these days. In case you hadn't noticed, I'm all grown-up now."

"Oh, I noticed," he said grimly. "I noticed all right."

IT WAS LATE by the time they decided to call it a night. They'd searched through the archives for hours, but they hadn't been able to locate any of the case files from the murders twenty years ago. The archives had been moved several years ago into a new building after the old facility had been damaged by fire. Elizabeth supposed it was possible the files had either been destroyed or lost, but it seemed odd no one had noticed they were missing until now.

She tried to remember everything she'd heard about the murders, but the only thing that stood out in her mind was the suspect. David Bryson. In the ensuing years, he'd become a wealthy man. Now he had enough money to protect himself from a police investigation, Elizabeth thought. To hide away in his fortress until the smoke cleared.

As they drove back toward Heathrow, Elizabeth laid her head against the seat and thought about the recent murder. About the lack of evidence and the lack of suspects. What they needed, she thought wearily, was a break in this case, and soon. Before the killer struck again.

The night was very dark, with heavy cloud coverage blocking the moon, and a pea-soup fog that had rolled in from the sea. Cullen drove cautiously, his frowning gaze on the road. He didn't speak. He appeared so deep in thought that Elizabeth wondered if he'd forgotten her presence entirely.

She turned her head on the seat, studying his features in the dash lights. His jaw was firmly set, his mouth thin, his eyes slightly narrowed as he watched the road. There'd always been something about him that girls were riveted to, even when he'd been considered a bad boy. And in truth, that had probably been part of his appeal. But now, even wearing a badge, even on the right side of the law, he was still very attractive. Maybe not as smooth and polished as Lucian LeCroix, but the rough edges and a faintly sinister past only emphasized his masculinity and made Elizabeth all the more drawn to him.

She thought about what she knew of his childhood. His mother had left the family when Cullen was only five or six, and he'd been raised by a father who'd spent long months at sea. Elizabeth had no idea who'd taken care of Cullen during his father's absences, but she had a feeling he'd pretty much been left to his own devices.

She supposed they had that in common, although she doubted Cullen would see it that way. She'd been brought up in the lap of luxury. She'd grown up in a beautiful home, raised by a nanny with impeccable credentials. No expense had been spared when it came to Elizabeth's physical well being and to her education. And yet the thing she remembered most about her childhood was the loneliness. The hours spent by herself, waiting…just waiting….

Had Cullen experienced that, too? That aching feeling in the pit of his stomach, that terrible suspicion that no one cared much whether he lived or died?

He turned suddenly and caught her watching him. "What?"

"What, what?"

He smiled. "I think we've had this conversation before. Why are you staring at me like that?"

Because I like looking at you, she wanted to tell him, but instead she shrugged. "I was just thinking about the case. Do you think it's possible Bethany's murder could be tied to those old killings?"

His expression turned grim. "All I know for certain at this point is that we're dealing with a real sicko."

Elizabeth stared out the window, trying to imagine what the killer was thinking. Was he cowering in terror since he'd killed Bethany? Was he wondering in horror how he could have done such a thing? *Why* he'd done such a thing? Was he panicking, feeling the authorities closing in on him?

Or was he holed up somewhere, savoring his conquest? Reliving past glories? Was he thrilled at the prospect of the next one? Planning even now who his next victim would be?

Elizabeth shivered as she watched the fog melt past her window, and she suddenly thought about Claire, about that night in the cemetery that had changed all of them forever. Claire had been taken by a monster, and in the days and nights that followed her abduction, she'd been subjected to a horror that only she could know. That she, herself, hadn't been able to live with.

She still breathed, still ate and slept, still dreamed perhaps, but her life had been stolen from her just as surely as Bethany Peters's life had been taken from her. Just as surely as Leslie Ridgemont's life and all the other victims' lives had been cut short twenty years ago.

Elizabeth tried to peer through the fog outside her window, and for a moment, she could have sworn invisible eyes were staring back at her.

"Do you believe in ghosts?" she asked softly. Her gaze was still on the window.

"No," Cullen said flatly. "Do you?"

She thought for a moment. "Yes, I think I do."

"You surprise me, Elizabeth."

She turned to face him. "Why?"

"Someone with your intelligence, and yet you've bought into all those old tales. They're just stories. They're not real."

"Myths are often based on facts," she reminded him.

He shot her an exasperated glance. "Do you honestly believe McFarland Leary rises from his grave every five years to terrorize Moriah's Landing?"

"He was supposed to have risen the night we went to the cemetery," she said, wrapping her arms around her middle. "And Claire was abducted."

"No ghost tortured that poor girl," Cullen said harshly. "No ghost killed Bethany Peters. There's a monster out there somewhere. I'll grant you that. But he's real. He's a flesh-and-blood man who can be taken down when we catch him. And we will catch him."

He glanced at her then, his expression stern in the dash lights. "There's no such thing as ghosts."

Elizabeth opened her mouth, to say what, she wasn't quite sure, but as she turned to stare out the windshield, the fog parted and she saw something in the road. Something wispy and fragile. Something that stared into the headlights, undaunted.

"Cullen, watch out!" she screamed.

Chapter Eleven

"What the hell—" Cullen saw him at the same time she did, and he braked so suddenly, Elizabeth would have shot through the windshield if not for her safety belt.

As the car rocked to a stop, she squeezed her eyes closed, bracing herself for the awful thud of flesh against metal. When no sound was forthcoming, she thought the specter must have passed cleanly through the car. She slit her eyes, hardly daring to find out.

But then she saw him standing in the hazy glare of the headlights, his features indistinct but very real.

Cullen reached for the door handle. "Wait here."

But Elizabeth had already opened her door, too, and she scrambled out. They hurried around to the front of the car where the man remained transfixed in the glow of the car's fog lights. He was dressed for the cold, in a heavy gray overcoat, hat, gloves and muffler. He appeared large, but Elizabeth thought the bulk of his clothing might be contributing to his size.

"Hey," Cullen said. "Are you okay? Did I hit you?"

"No, no. The car didn't touch me." His voice was cultured, but there was something oddly disturbing about it, a quality that sounded almost…otherworldly, for lack of a better term. Elizabeth found herself shivering in the misty cold.

"I was just out for a stroll," he said in a conversational tone. "I must have gotten caught up in my thoughts, and I didn't see the headlights. Sorry to frighten you."

"Out for a stroll?" Cullen said. "Hardly a great night for walking, is it?"

"Oh, I don't mind the cold. Or the fog. Gives one a marvelous sense of isolation. Besides, the fresh air helps me to think."

"Maybe you should *think* about staying out of the middle of the road in fog this thick," Cullen said dryly. "I'm Detective Ryan with the Moriah's Landing Police Department. Mind showing me some identification?"

"Identification?" He patted his coat pocket. "I left my wallet at home, I'm afraid. I don't live far from here. My name is Leland Manning."

"*Dr.* Manning?" Elizabeth asked in surprise.

"Why, yes." He turned to her then, and although she couldn't see his expression clearly in the darkness, she had a feeling his eyes were deep and probing. That he was searching her own features and missing nothing. "Do I know you?"

"I'm Elizabeth Douglas. I believe you know my parents, Marion and Edward Douglas."

He peered at her through the mist. "Ah. I see the resemblance now. An extraordinary woman, your mother. As brilliant as she is beautiful."

"Thank you," Elizabeth murmured, discomfited by the man's piercing gaze.

"You say you live around here?" Cullen asked him.

Manning turned. "Yes. Not far from the college."

"Maybe we should give you a lift. Probably not a good idea to be out here walking around by yourself."

"Oh, I'll be careful," Manning assured him. "The night air helps to clear my head after I've been in the laboratory all day."

"That may be," Cullen said. "But if I were you, I'd take my walks before dark. At least for a while."

Manning nodded. "I understand what you're saying, Detective. You're referring to that student who was recently murdered. You haven't found her killer yet, have you?"

"We're working on it," Cullen assured him. "It's only a matter of time."

Manning shook his head. "She was a lovely girl. Such a pity." He turned, his gaze meeting Elizabeth's in the darkness. "All that potential, wasted."

"THAT IS one seriously weird dude," Cullen muttered as they drove away.

Elizabeth craned her neck to watch behind them until the fog had swallowed up Leland Manning. Then she turned back around, shivering. "He has a rather Hannibal Lector-ish quality about him, doesn't he?"

"He does kind of look like that guy who plays Lector in the movies." Cullen glanced at Elizabeth. "I take it you know him?"

"Only by reputation. His name is legendary in the scientific community. He was one of the pioneers of gene therapy research."

Cullen watched the road, but Elizabeth saw him glance periodically in the rearview mirror, as if he expected Manning to materialize suddenly in the back seat. "Gene therapy?"

"Yes. It's a way to correct certain diseases at their root. Essentially, there are two forms. One is called somatic gene therapy which involves the manipulation of gene expression in cells that will be corrective to the patient but not inherited by the next generation. The other form is called germline gene therapy, which involves the genetic modification of germ cells that will pass the change on to the next generation. You're getting into some tricky territory there, ethically speaking."

"Sounds like something from the sci-fi station if you ask me," Cullen said. "So Manning is involved in all this monkeying around with genes?"

Elizabeth nodded. "Yes, but there's more. He has a rather bizarre theory about witches."

"Witches? Why do I suddenly feel as if I'm in the Twilight Zone?" Cullen grumbled.

"Manning has a pet theory that witches did, and do, have special powers, but it has nothing to do with black magic. He thinks some people are born with a special gene which, in some cases, gives them supernatural abilities."

Cullen rubbed the back of his neck. "He actually believes in this hocus pocus?"

"So he says." Absently Elizabeth tapped her chin with her fingertip. "It seems like there's something about him I should remember."

Cullen shot her a glance. "He's not secretly a werewolf or something, is he?"

Elizabeth grinned. "Nothing quite that interesting.

Some kind of scandal associated with him," she mused. "It happened a few years ago. I'm not certain of the timeline, but it involved another scientist. Manning's protégé, I believe. He had an odd name." She thought for a moment. "Rathfastar. Dr. René Rathfastar."

Cullen shot her a glance. "What the hell kind of name is that?"

"Shush. I'm trying to remember exactly what happened. As I recall, they were both working at the time on the Human Genome Project, but there were rumors they were both affiliated with some sort of secret society whose methodology wasn't endorsed by the mainstream scientific community. To put it bluntly, members of the society didn't necessarily concern themselves with the ethical and moral dilemmas that bedevil most legitimate research into human DNA."

"What kind of secret society are we talking about here?" Cullen's gaze looked skeptical. "You mean skull and crossbones type stuff?"

"More like a scientific Trilateral Commission," Elizabeth told him. "I've heard rumors that the membership contains some pretty powerful scientists. But, of course, it *is* just a rumor. I'm not at all certain such an organization really exists. It could be just another legend. Supposedly, however, the society dates back to the 1600s, when a group of scientists banded together to perform secret experiments on witches."

"And Manning is a member of this group?"

Elizabeth nodded. "According to local gossip. As was Dr. Rathfastar. And, come to think of it, so was Geoffrey Pierce."

Cullen turned. "What's Pierce got to do with all this?"

"I don't know that he does these days, but he used to be a wannabe scientist who used his family money and influence to buy his way into some important research projects. However, he never published any important findings."

"What about David Bryson? He's some kind of scientist, too, isn't he?"

"I never heard his name linked to the society, so I don't know." Elizabeth wondered if Cullen was thinking what she was thinking. All the men they'd just mentioned would have the know-how, as well as the equipment, to have performed such a grisly procedure on Bethany Peters. But where was the motive?

"I've gone up to Bryson's place to try and talk to him a couple of times, but that butler of his is pretty protective," Cullen said. "He wouldn't let me in."

"You think Bryson had something to do with Bethany's murder?"

"He was a suspect twenty years ago. A lot of people in town still have strong feelings about him." Cullen reached over and adjusted the controls on the heater. "But forget Bryson for the time being. Tell me what else you remember about Manning."

Elizabeth frowned in concentration. "There was some controversy regarding his research. Dr. Rathfastar accused Manning of publishing stolen findings, and Manning, in turn, claimed Rathfastar was a dangerous fanatic who used human test subjects in his research."

"Wow. A regular Dr. Frankenstein," Cullen commented dryly.

But Elizabeth barely heard him. She was remembering something else about Manning. An image came to her suddenly—her mother and father late one night sitting at the kitchen table. Elizabeth had come down for a drink of water and was surprised to find them there, in such a cozy, domestic setting. She'd wanted very much to join them, to tell them about her day or to simply sit quietly and listen while they talked.

But their low, angry tones kept her at bay, and she'd listened unabashedly at the door.

I've never made any secret of my feelings, Edward. You know I've always believed Leland Manning to be a fraud. A dangerous one at that.

For God's sake, Marion, you can't really mean that. The man is a genius. His research into the human genome is nothing short of phenomenal.

Research that he stole from his own colleagues. Her mother's tone grew acid.

Her father was silent for a moment, then he said angrily, "So that's it. You're taking his side."

"I'm not taking anyone's side, but I'm entitled to my own opinion. I happen to believe René."

"So it's René now, is it?" There was something in her father's voice that frightened Elizabeth.

"Oh, for God's sake, Edward, don't be ridiculous. The man is a colleague. What would you have me call him?"

"I don't give a damn what you call him. Just never mention his name in my presence again."

The memory spun away, and Elizabeth felt gooseflesh prickle on the back of her neck, as if she'd inadvertently remembered something forbidden.

"Elizabeth?"

Cullen's voice roused her from the past. "I'm sorry. I was just thinking. What did you say?"

"What happened to this Rathfastar character?"

She shrugged. "He just disappeared. For a while, I think there were whispers among their colleagues that Manning might have done him in, but then someone saw Rathfastar in Europe. In Brussels, I believe. Then later it was learned that he'd been in a terrible car accident and wasn't expected to live."

"Did he?"

Elizabeth shook her head. "I don't know. After the rumors died down, I never heard his name mentioned again." Certainly not at home.

"I still say all this sounds like something from a bad sci-fi movie."

"Well, it's not," she assured him. "Gene therapy and genetic engineering are here. So is cloning. The human race is going to have to find a way to deal with the moral and ethical dilemmas that will inevitably follow."

Cullen shot her a glance. "If it's all the same to you, I'd just as soon stick with the murder."

THE GUARD at the gate hurried over to the car and peered in the window. Cullen rolled down the glass, and the man shone his light inside the car.

"Dr. Douglas? That you?"

"Good evening, George."

The guard flicked off the flashlight and glanced from Elizabeth to Cullen, frowning. "Out kind of late in this weather, aren't you?"

"I'm in good company, George. You remember Detective Ryan."

"Sure do." George's gaze was disapproving. "Are you here on official business?"

"Just dropping Dr. Douglas off at her place." An

edge of impatience crept into Cullen's voice. "How about opening those gates for us?"

George wasn't one for being told how to do his job. He hesitated, and for a moment, Elizabeth thought he might actually refuse. He was only thirty-five or so, but a rounding middle and a balding pate gave him an older appearance. He'd been around for as long as Elizabeth could remember, and he took his job very seriously.

"You take care, Dr. Douglas," he finally said. He went back to the guardhouse and pressed the control so that the heavy, iron gates slid open.

Cullen stepped on the gas and the car shot through the opening before the gates had fully extended. "That guy's kind of protective of you, isn't he?"

"George? He's always been that way."

"How long has he worked here?"

Elizabeth shrugged. "Forever, it seems."

"Know anything about his background?"

"Not really, but I'm sure he has an employee file in the administration office. But for heaven's sakes, Cullen, you can't really suspect George. He's harmless."

"Is he?"

Was he? How much did Elizabeth really know about George Wiley? How much did she know about anyone at Heathrow? Or anyone in town for that matter?

But George? He'd always been so nice to her. Always looked out for her.

Elizabeth remembered once when he'd caught her and Kat climbing the tree branches on the southwest side of the campus to scale the wall after curfew. He'd read them the riot act, but he hadn't written them up, for which Elizabeth had been grateful. But Kat had scoffed at the gesture. "He's just trying to impress you. I think he has a little crush on you," she'd teased. After that night, Kat had dubbed him the Gate Nazi. "I wouldn't be surprised if he's planted a few hidden cameras in the dorms."

"Kat! George wouldn't do that. He's a nice man."

"Oh, grow up, Elizabeth. You're so naive. Everybody knows the man's a perv."

Elizabeth hated to think that her perception of someone could be that far off base.

Cullen pulled into a parking space and killed the engine. When he came around to open her door, he even went so far as to put out a hand to her. Elizabeth took it, feeling the warmth of his flesh against hers. Feeling all tingly with anticipation.

She'd hadn't left a light on in the house, but there was a security light at the edge of her tiny yard and another one in the tiny green directly across from her house. She could see Cullen's features only faintly as he walked her to her door.

Elizabeth leaned against the frame, suddenly shy. "It's a cold night. Do you want to come in for a cup of tea?"

He hesitated. "I'd better be going."

He leaned down suddenly, and for one breathless moment, Elizabeth thought he was going to kiss her. Everything stilled inside her as she waited. As she wanted.

But instead, he lifted a hand to gently brush against her cheek. "You've still got a bruise. I noticed it the other day."

"I got it at the funeral home." Elizabeth unconsciously lifted her hand to the spot, and their fingers brushed, entangled. She closed her eyes briefly at the contact.

He leaned in, planting his other hand on the doorframe above her head. "I shouldn't do this."

Elizabeth swallowed. "Do what?"

"Kiss you."

"Oh." She swallowed again and barely had time to draw a breath before Cullen's lips brushed against hers. Softly. Curiously. Cautiously.

He lifted his head. "Are you going to slap my face?"

Hardly.

She shook her head.

For the longest moment, their gazes held. Then he kissed her again, and this time there was nothing curious or cautious about the action. His mouth pressed against hers, moving slowly back and forth until Elizabeth's lips parted eagerly, and she heard herself sigh.

She'd dreamed about this moment so often she hardly dared to believe it was real. But it was. It was! Cullen Ryan was kissing her so passionately she couldn't think straight. Couldn't breathe properly. And it was everything she'd thought it would be and more.

All these years, when Elizabeth had held herself aloof from passion, she'd pretended that she wasn't saving herself for the right man so much as the right moment. The time for love simply hadn't presented itself. But now, with Cullen's lips on hers, with his fingers threading through her hair, shaking loose the prim bun at her nape, Elizabeth knew she'd been deluding herself.

She hadn't been saving herself for the right moment. She'd been saving herself for Cullen. Only Cullen.

He pulled away, his eyes dark and mysterious in the filtered light. "You shouldn't be doing this with a guy like me."

"What do you mean?" she asked breathlessly.

"You know exactly what I mean."

"Cullen—"

"There's a lot about my past I'm not proud of, Elizabeth."

"Regret isn't unique to you," she murmured.

He lifted a hand to tuck a strand of hair behind her ear. "What have you got to regret?" When she didn't answer, his expression sobered. "I'm not looking for a serious involvement right now. With anyone."

Her heart sank a bit. "Who says I am?"

He studied her for a moment. "Then what do you want from me, Elizabeth?"

"I…just want you to kiss me again."

He looked surprised. Then he laughed a little. "I can do that."

And he did. He kissed her over and over, until everything faded from Elizabeth's mind except the heat of his mouth on hers. Until her knees grew weak and she felt all quivery inside. Until her desire for Cullen almost overwhelmed her.

She'd never experienced this before. Never been kissed this way. Never wanted to go that final step as badly as she wanted to now.

Cullen drew away, looking a bit dazed himself. "Wow. You're just full of surprises, aren't you?"

"Am I?"

He laughed again. "Damn right. I wasn't expecting this from you, Elizabeth."

"What? That I know how to kiss?"

"That you'd want to, I guess."

"I'm not a prude."

"I'm beginning to get that message." He trailed a finger along her jawline, and Elizabeth shivered. "It's cold out. I should let you go in."

She wasn't the least bit cold. "You could come in, too," she suggested shyly.

"No," Cullen said firmly. "I can't. Not tonight."

"Why not?"

"Let's not rush this, okay? One step at a time." He kissed her again, and then he was gone.

Chapter Twelve

Everything changed after that night.

Before Cullen had kissed her, Elizabeth had thought they were cultivating an important relationship. He'd taken a big step in coming to ask for her help, and she'd believed it to be an encouraging sign that after all this time, he was finally realizing she'd grown up. He was finally seeing her in a new light.

But after that night, his whole attitude toward her changed. To put it simply, he started avoiding her.

Part of it, she decided, was his very real belief that he wasn't the right man for her. But she also suspected he was scared of caring for someone because of the way he'd been brought up.

Elizabeth knew what it was like to feel abandoned. To be so hurt and lonely you felt as though you didn't have a soul in the world who cared about you. Eventually, you grew defensive. You erected a wall around your heart. You tried in every way you knew how to make yourself invincible to hurt and disappointment.

She knew all about that.

But she was willing to take the risk. She was tired of being lonely. She wanted someone to love and to love her in return. She wanted a home and family. She wanted Cullen.

It didn't matter to her that they were young and that statistics worked against them. What mattered to her was that they would have each other.

But, Cullen, of course, didn't see it that way. He saw their burgeoning feelings as some kind of trap.

Oh, he'd called her the next day as he'd promised, but even then, the conversation had been strictly business, with no reference whatsoever to what had happened between them the night before. And his tone had been stilted and reluctant. Elizabeth had known at once that he was pulling away. As the weeks went by, it became even more obvious.

But in spite of his aloofness, Elizabeth remained active on the case. She'd received a copy of the autopsy report, and she'd pored over the pages time and again, searching for something that she and Cullen might have missed. She studied the crime-scene photos and the witness interviews, and during the week of spring break, when the campus was all but deserted and she had some free time on her hands, she made a chart, listing all the suspects, their possible motives and their whereabouts, if known, on the night she'd discovered Bethany's body.

She went over that list now in her mind. First was Geoffrey Pierce, not because she believed him to be the chief suspect, but because his actions that night had inspired a certain unease. He hadn't seemed the least bit shocked or disturbed to see the body of a young woman hanging in his brother's solarium. And he had a scientific background, which spoke, not only to the test tube she and Cullen had found in the cooler room at the mortuary, but to the procedure that had been performed on Bethany.

Next came Lucian LeCroix because, whether Elizabeth wanted to believe it or not, Cullen was right. No one in Moriah's Landing really knew much about him. Elizabeth suspected that Cullen, given his initial dislike of the man, had made a few calls to some of his old buddies in the Boston Police Department, trying to dig up whatever he could on Lucian, but if he'd heard anything suspicious, he hadn't seen fit to share.

She put Ned Krauter, the undertaker, on the list for obvious reasons. And because he was creepy. He talked to dead people. Not a motive that would hold up in court, to be sure, but Elizabeth wasn't willing to leave any stone unturned.

Beside Paul Fortier's name, she drew a tiny star, signifying a very strong suspect. He'd known Bethany, and though they'd found no evidence so far indicating a personal relationship between the two, Elizabeth didn't discount the possibility. Plus, Fortier had acted as if he had something to hide that day in the lab, not to mention the blood he'd been working with, and the tear in his lab coat, which seemed suspicious. Without any physical evidence or eyewitness testimony linking him to the murder—in other words, without probable cause—neither the blood nor his records could be confiscated so they remained in the dark as to the nature of his experiments. But even if the blood had been Bethany's, he would have long since disposed of it.

As an afterthought, Elizabeth included Leland Manning's name on the list. Manning was a long shot, but like Ned Krauter, there was something about him that unnerved her. And again, his scientific background came into play, not to mention his bizarre theory about witches. Had someone drained Bethany's body of blood for experimental purposes? For some dark sacrifice? Or simply for sick pleasure?

"Checkmate!"

The delighted voice jolted Elizabeth out of her reverie. She glanced down to see that her four-year-old brother, Brandon, had thoroughly trounced her at chess.

She frowned. "That's impossible."

"No, it's not. I won!" he cried gleefully. "I won! I won! I won!"

"All right," she admonished. "It's not nice to gloat."

"Sorry," he said, chastised, but his eyes gleamed with pleasure, and Elizabeth couldn't help smiling. He was adorable, with his glossy black hair and light blue eyes, so striking against his dark coloring. Not only was his IQ several points higher than hers had been at his age, but he'd gotten all the looks in the family as well.

"Can we play again? I bet you'll win this time." All the charm as well.

Elizabeth reached over and mussed his hair. "Afraid not. It's way past your bedtime. If you're not under the covers in two minutes, Annie will come up here and have both our hides," she said, referring to Brandon's nanny.

He heaved a sigh. "Okay. But will you read me a story?"

"Why, you little con artist," Elizabeth accused him, tucking him in. "I gave you a choice between a story and chess, and you chose chess. And besides, you're perfectly capable of reading a story on your own.''

''I know.'' Those beautiful eyes, framed with long, sooty lashes, stared up at her solemnly. ''But I love the way you read, 'Lizbeth. It makes me have the nicest dreams.''

How could she resist that? ''Well, okay.'' She walked over to the bookcase to select a title. ''But just for a few minutes. And then it's lights out. No arguments.''

He signed a cross on his chest. ''I promise.''

Elizabeth made a production of searching through his books. ''What'll it be tonight?'' As if she had to ask.

''Indiana Jones!'' he shrieked.

She cut him a glance. ''Don't you ever get tired of hearing about all those dark, creepy places crawling with spiders and snakes and goodness knows what.'' She faked a shudder.

He laughed, a little-boy sound that belied his often-serious disposition. ''I like dark, creepy places. I'm going to be an archeologist when I grow up.''

Don't let Mother and Father hear you say that. Elizabeth smiled encouragingly. ''You can be anything you want when you grow up. You just have to follow your own dreams. Not someone else's. Okay?''

He nodded, anxious for her to begin the story. On impulse, she leaned over and kissed his cheek.

He rubbed the spot with his fingertips. ''Why'd you do that?''

''Because I wanted to. And in case you fall asleep before we finish the story.''

"Good idea. But don't worry. I won't fall asleep," he assured her.

Elizabeth couldn't help but smile. She was barely into the second page when he began to nod off. She tucked him in, kissed him again, and then turned off his light before tiptoeing from his room.

Downstairs, she noticed a light underneath her mother's office door, and wondered if both her parents had come in while she'd been upstairs with Brandon. If so, they hadn't seen fit to come up and say good-night to their young son, but that was no surprise. Bedtime stories and good-night hugs were part of the nanny's duties.

Elizabeth wondered, as she'd wondered a thousand times before, why her parents had had children only to delegate their care to strangers. But she knew the answer only too well. Marion and Edward Douglas were both brilliant; their offspring would do amazing things for humankind. But Elizabeth hadn't exactly been willing to mold herself to their expectations. She suspected that was why they'd decided to have Brandon so late in life.

Hesitating, she walked over and knocked on her mother's door.

Silence, and then an impatient, "Yes?"

"Mother, it's Elizabeth. May I come in for a minute?"

"Elizabeth? Is something wrong?"

Elizabeth opened the door and stepped into her mother's office. Even at her age, she felt a bit intimidated. This room had been a forbidden place to her as a child, as had her father's study, which was located in the back of the house. She could probably count on both hands the number of times she'd been allowed inside this office, and now, as she gazed around, she realized she hadn't missed a thing. The word *sterile* came to mind. Nothing on the walls, on the desk, or in the bookcases to give away even one little hint of her mother's personality. It was all about her work.

Marion Douglas was seated behind her desk, and in the glow of her computer screen, she looked hardly more than twenty herself, certainly not old enough to have a grown daughter. In her mid-forties, she was still a beautiful woman, with hair a little darker than Elizabeth's and eyes more green than hazel. But there was still a strong resemblance between them, and it struck Elizabeth again how odd it was that they could look so much alike and be so different.

Brandon, on the other hand, didn't resemble Marion or Edward. He had his own unique looks, his own special personality, and Elizabeth thought it was a pity that her parents didn't seem to appreciate just how wonderful their son truly was. He was not only a genius, but a sweet, good-natured child. A blessing.

"Elizabeth?" Her mother sounded annoyed. "*Is* something wrong?"

"No, nothing's wrong."

"Then what are you doing here?"

Did she need a reason? Elizabeth tamped down the old hurt. "I came to have dinner with Brandon."

"Oh." Her mother shrugged. "Well, I assume Doris took good care of you."

Yes, Elizabeth thought. The housekeeper had done her job well. The meal had been perfectly cooked, perfectly served at the perfectly appointed table in the perfectly decorated dining room. She and Brandon had sat alone at the large table while the dour-faced

Doris served them. Elizabeth had enjoyed the meal in spite of their austere surroundings simply because she loved spending time with her brother.

But she couldn't help thinking what it was like for him when she wasn't there. When he sat alone at that table. Just as she had once sat alone.

She took a seat across from her mother's desk, refusing for once in her life to be intimidated by Marion's brusque manner. "I need to talk to you about something."

"I'm busy—"

"This won't take long."

At her insistent tone, her mother looked up from the computer screen with a frown. "What is it?"

"How well do you know Leland Manning?"

"Manning?" Her mother stared at her for a moment. "Why on earth do you want to know about Leland Manning?"

Elizabeth shrugged. "Because I ran into him the other night, and the incident reminded me of something I overheard you and Father talking about once. Some sort of scandal associated with Manning."

"I'm sure I don't know anything about a scandal." Her mother turned back to her work, but in the glow of the monitor, Elizabeth saw that her features had tightened. That her mouth had thinned with displeasure.

"Yes, you do," Elizabeth persisted. "It involved that secret society of scientists to which both Manning and his protégé supposedly belonged. Is it coming back to you now?"

Her mother hesitated, busying herself at the keyboard. Then she turned off the screen, and her face suddenly looked its age in the harsh glare of the desk lamp. "I don't know anything about a secret society. It sounds like something you must have dreamed up, Elizabeth." But her tone sounded strained, as if Elizabeth had struck a nerve.

"Do you remember what happened between Manning and the other scientist? His name was René Rathfastar, I think."

It was as if a switch had been flipped, not just on the computer screen, but on Marion Douglas's face. Her features seemed almost frozen. "Why all these questions?"

"I told you. I ran into Manning the other night, and now I'm curious about him. And about Rathfastar. They had some kind of falling out, right? Rathfastar moved to Europe, to Brussels, wasn't it?"

"I really wouldn't know."

Her mother's expression was fascinating to watch. Elizabeth had never seen so many conflicting emotions flit across Marion's face. "He was in a terrible car accident. Do you know if he survived?"

"How would I know that?"

"Mother, you and Father and Manning—and Rathfastar, if he's still alive—all work in the same field. You must remember what happened between them. You must have heard whether Rathfastar survived that car crash. Why are you being so evasive?"

Marion's eyes flashed with sudden anger. "The only thing I can tell you is that Leland Manning is a very cunning man. He is not at all what he pretends to be. A word to the wise, Elizabeth. Stay as far away from that megalomaniac as you possibly can." She turned her monitor back on then, and instantly grew absorbed in something on the screen. Her face became a blank slate, the emotions once again tucked away into a compartment where they couldn't interfere with her work. Elizabeth knew further questions would be useless.

Outside the office, she paused, unsettled by the conversation and by her mother's prevarication. Why had she been so unwilling to talk about Manning and Rathfastar? And about the secret society, for that matter? Unless, of course, she and Elizabeth's father were both members?

But Elizabeth found that hard to believe. Their work was their lives. She couldn't imagine either of them being affiliated with any organization which might jeopardize their reputations and their research.

Then why had her mother been so evasive?

And in another flash of memory, something came to Elizabeth that had been niggling at her for days, ever since she'd seen Leland Manning.

Five years ago, just after Elizabeth had moved on campus at Heathrow, her mother had left rather suddenly for a conference in Brussels.

"YOU ALL BY yourself tonight, Dr. Douglas?" George shone his flashlight beam inside her car, as if expecting to see someone pop up from the back seat.

"Just me tonight, George."

He flicked off the light. "Well, you take care, you hear? This place is like a graveyard tonight. Everyone gone but you and me. You need anything, you give me a shout."

"I will. Thanks, George."

As the gates clamored open, Elizabeth pulled through, shivering a bit at George's comparison to a graveyard. There *was* something a bit spooky about a school campus during spring break, she decided.

The place was so quiet she could almost hear ghost laughter.

Parking in her regular spot, Elizabeth got out and hurried up the walkway to her house. The weather had been nice for the last few days, heating up to a balmy fifty degrees during the day. But with the warmer weather, a low-lying fog had rolled in from the sea, undulating like some giant sea creature beneath the security lights.

Entering her house, Elizabeth closed and bolted the front door, and then paused, listening to the deep quiet of the deserted campus. Nothing spooky about it, she decided. If anything, it was calm and peaceful. Just the sort of night for a hot shower and an early bedtime. And maybe a little reading once she was snuggled safely underneath the covers.

She stood under the hot water for several long moments, hoping the sting of the spray would help alleviate a mild depression that had settled over her since her visit with her mother. Actually, the depression had started weeks ago, when Cullen had started avoiding her.

Walking into her closet, she grabbed one of her cotton nightgowns from a hanger, but then seeing the filmy negligee set her friend and fellow teacher, Rada Kilmeade, had given her for Christmas, Elizabeth chose it instead. She'd been saving the set for a special occasion, but at the rate she was going, she would die a weathered old virgin who would have no need of sexy lingerie. Might as well enjoy it while she could.

She slipped the silky white fabric over her head, and then selected a book from the collection she kept under lock and key in her bedroom. She was just about to crawl into bed when a noise brought her up short.

Standing perfectly still, she listened to the silence. When she heard nothing else, Elizabeth told herself she was imagining things. But with a killer roaming free and the campus all but abandoned, she couldn't ignore even an invented sound.

Pulling on the matching robe, she walked into the living room, pausing once again at the door to listen. She was just about to give up and head off to bed when the sound came again. Something faint. Something out of place.

Whistling, she thought. Someone was outside her cottage whistling.

George, no doubt, making his nightly rounds.

Elizabeth expelled a long breath of relief, and even considered opening the door to call out to the guard when she thought better of it. Instead, she crossed to the window and pulled back the drapes to stare out.

She saw nothing at first. Ground mist glowed with a strange yellowish tint beneath the security lights and obscured much of the scenery. But across from her house, something moved on the tiny green. A shadow...

Elizabeth peered through the darkness. Not a shadow, she thought. Something was hanging from a tree branch, swaying in a slight breeze. A body—

Her heart slammed against her chest as her hand flew to her mouth.

Her first instinct was to rush out and see if she could help, but then she remembered the whistle, realized the killer could still be near. He might have made the noise deliberately to draw her outside.

The phone!

She whirled, lunging toward her desk, but before she was halfway across the room, she heard another sound.

This time not a whistle.

This time closer.

This time in her house.

She wasn't alone, she realized with a dreadful certainty that threatened her knees. That made a scream rise up in her throat. Her instincts took over then, and she spun, rushing toward the front door, throwing it open and plunging into the night.

She ran heedlessly. Blindly. Not knowing at first where she was going, just away from her house. Away from the killer.

When she saw her car materialize in the parking lot in front of her, she realized there had been a method to her madness. But her keys were in her purse, and her purse was on her desk, next to the phone....

The sound of footsteps on the cobblestone walkway brought her sharply around. The mist swirled and writhed. Someone was coming. The killer—

Her pulse thundering in her ears, Elizabeth turned again and headed for the gates. George would be in the guardhouse, and he had a telephone. He also had a weapon. They could lock themselves in until the police arrived.

She was gasping for breath by this time. The terror had winded her, but Elizabeth knew she had to keep going. The bedroom slippers impeded her speed, but she didn't dare take the time to kick them off. She ran. She ran until she thought her lungs would burst and her legs would collapse beneath her. When she saw the guardhouse ahead of her, she let out a sob of relief.

She couldn't see George, but he had to be inside. He had to be! She pounded on the glass. "Please!" she cried frantically. "Open up!"

But it was no use. It was after eleven, and George would be out making his rounds. The telephone was locked tightly inside the guardhouse, as was the control to activate the gates. Without access to the guardhouse or to the remote control she kept in her car, Elizabeth was trapped inside the campus. The gates were at least twelve feet high, the stone wall eight. No way she could scale it—

The southwest corner! Where tree branches dipped low over the wall. Where Kat had taught her how to sneak in and out after curfew.

Elizabeth ran through the darkness, wondering frantically if there was anyone at all left on campus except her and the killer. Would it do any good to scream? Even if someone was around, they might not hear her. Or they might not find her in time. All she might end up doing was alerting the killer to her whereabouts.

The tree branches were higher than she remembered, and Elizabeth's heart sank in despair. She didn't know if she could reach them. Before, she'd had Kat to give her a hand up or a boost from the ground. Now she had no one.

Come on! She could almost hear Kat coaxing her. *You can do this! Now, get your butt up here. Jump!*

She missed completely the first time. The second time, her fingertips brushed against the bark. The third time, she managed to grab hold of the branch, clinging with all her might while her feet swung wildly and she grunted from the effort.

Steeling her resolve, she dug in, using the adrenaline rush of her fear to give her the strength to swing her body up, to wrap her legs around the branch, to crawl along the limb until she reached the wall. Up and over, and then drop to the ground below.

She landed on her backside, but Elizabeth didn't take time to worry about injuries. She was up and running through the trees to the road. From there, it was still a mile to the police station, but surely a car would come along before that. Or she would find a telephone.

Through the hushed mist came the unmistakable sound of metal scraping against metal. The front gates were opening, and then, a second later, she heard the roar of a car engine as it thundered through. Elizabeth prayed that the killer would guess wrong and head north, away from her location. But she could hear the sound of the engine getting stronger by the second. Gaining on her.

The killer was coming for her. Somehow, he'd known where she would be.

She had to get off the road.

Glancing around to get her bearings, Elizabeth hurried across the pavement and struck out through the woods. She knew Leland Manning's house and laboratory were around there somewhere, but his property was surrounded by an electronic fence. There would be no getting inside unless she could make it to the front gate and press the intercom button, pray that someone was home.

But did she really want to do that? What if Manning was the killer?

In the mist and darkness, it was difficult to keep a sense of direction, but Elizabeth tried her best to skirt Manning's property. When she finally came out on another road, she realized finally where she was. If Leland Manning's property was behind her, St. John's Cemetery was just ahead, on the opposite side of the road. If she headed straight through the graveyard, she would come out near Old Mountain Road, which would put miles between her and Heathrow, and hopefully the killer. It would also bring her near the Bluffs, but Elizabeth wasn't at all certain she wanted to seek refuge with David Bryson any more than she did with Leland Manning.

Hearing the low rumble of a car engine fired her into action. She ran across the road, searching for the gates that would open into the cemetery. Whether David Bryson was the killer or not, she couldn't waste time worrying. She had to get to a phone.

Spotting the gates, she rushed toward them. The metal opened with a screech, and Elizabeth hurried through.

She hadn't been in St. John's Cemetery since the night of the sorority initiation. Now, huddling just inside the walls, she gazed around in mounting agitation. The cemetery had been eerie and menacing in the storm, but the mist was even creepier. It swirled and slid among the headstones, draped the mausoleums in a filmy shroud until only the tops could be seen.

Elizabeth hurried along, trying not to step on graves, hoping not to disturb the dead. Cullen had said he didn't believe in ghosts, and she wanted to take comfort in his certainty. But the trouble was, she did believe in the supernatural. She did believe in spirits.

From somewhere behind her, the gates clanged softly. Elizabeth knew instinctively the killer had entered the cemetery, and her situation suddenly seemed hopeless. She'd been running all this time while he'd been behind the wheel of a car. She was exhausted from the hunt; he would be fresh, exhilarated. There was no way she could outrun him. The best thing to do was find a hiding place, pray that her nightgown and robe would blend with the mist.

She crouched behind a headstone, pressing herself against the cool surface as she listened to the night. She could hear him coming. He was breathing heavily, but not from exertion. From excitement. From anticipation. From the thrill of the hunt.

Or was the sound her imagination? A figment of her fear?

She didn't dare glance around the headstone. She knelt there for long, excruciating moments until finally she heard the gates screech again. He had left the way he'd come in. Or at least, he wanted her to think he had.

Elizabeth didn't know what to do. She couldn't hide there forever. If he was still in the cemetery, searching for her, he would find her eventually. She had to get out.

Standing on shaky legs, she glanced around. She hadn't noticed before, but she was only a few feet from the mausoleum where Claire had been abducted. Elizabeth recognized the broken cross on top. That meant that McFarland Leary's grave was around here somewhere.

She stared in the direction she thought his headstone should be. The mist over his grave swirled. Contorted. Reshaped itself into—she would have sworn—a human form.

A scream bubbled up inside her, and Elizabeth clapped a hand over her mouth to snuff the sound. She whirled, running recklessly through the foggy night, not knowing where she was headed or where she would end up, but miraculously, the second set of gates opened up before her. The hinges screamed in protest when she pushed them open, and then she raced through, running in terror as if the devil himself were pursuing her. And for all she knew he was.

Her first indication of yet a new danger was her feet hitting pavement. She was on a road. Elizabeth paused, looked up, and saw headlights plowing through the fog toward her.

He'd found her! The killer had found her!

Momentarily paralyzed with fear, she watched the lights rushing toward her. The sound of the car engine was a death roar in her ears.

At the last moment, when she could feel the motor's heat, Elizabeth found her senses and dove for the side of the road.

The car squealed to a stop, a door slammed and footsteps hurried across the pavement.

Elizabeth tried to run, but her legs would no longer carry her. She huddled in the mist as the killer strode toward her.

Chapter Thirteen

"Elizabeth!"

She was so scared and so stunned that for a moment, her brain couldn't assimilate the sound of her name being called by—not the killer—someone she trusted with her life.

Then, when she saw him hurrying toward her through the fog, she launched herself at him. "Cullen!"

He caught her by the arms and then, feeling her tremble, pulled her against him, holding her close. "Elizabeth? What's wrong? What's happened? What are you doing out here at this time of night?"

She was still shaking so badly she could hardly speak. She buried her face in his shoulder, drinking in the scent of him, the comfort of him. "He's...out there. In the cemetery."

He stiffened. "Who's out there?"

"The killer."

He pushed her gently away then, holding her at arms' length as he bent and peered into her face. "Elizabeth. What are you saying?"

"The killer is in the cemetery. Or he was. There's another body...I saw her...."

Cullen's grip on her tightened. "Where?"

"At Heathrow. In the green by my house. She's...hanging from a tree branch."

"Come on." He hurried her over to his car and helped her inside, then he ran around and got behind the wheel. Pulling the car to the side of the road, he turned to face her. "Tell me what happened. Everything." Noticing that she was still shivering, he turned on the heater full blast.

"Lock the doors," she whispered desperately.

"They're locked. Now tell me what happened. As quickly as you can."

"I'd just gotten out of the shower, and I heard a noise. Someone whistling. I looked out the window, and I saw her hanging in the tree. I started to call the police, call you, and then I heard something else. He was in my house, so I ran."

"You ran all the way from Heathrow to here?" he asked incredulously.

She nodded. "When you stopped just now, I thought you were the killer. He was in a car...."

"Did you see the car?"

She shook her head.

"You didn't see him?"

"No."

Cullen unlocked the glove box and removed a small-caliber weapon. Thumbing off the safety, he placed it on the console between them. "All you have to do is point and shoot."

She stared at him in alarm. "What are you going to do?"

"Have a look around the cemetery."

She clutched his arm. "You can't. He could still be out there."

"And if he is, we can't let him go free." Cullen's features hardened. "We can't let him kill again."

He removed his gun from his shoulder holster and checked the clip. Then he placed his cell phone in her hand and curled her fingers around it. "Call headquarters. Tell them you're with me. Tell them what happened. We need officers over here and at the college. They'll probably need to call in the state police for backup. Can you do that?"

"Of course, but Cullen—" She gripped his arm, unwilling to let him go into the cemetery alone. She was terrified he would never come back out. "I'm scared."

"Yeah, well, that makes two of us," he said with a tense smile.

FORTY-FIVE MINUTES later they were back at Heathrow. Officers from both the Moriah's Landing Police Department and the Massachusetts State Police were combing through St. John's Cemetery and the woods surrounding Leland Manning's property. Additional officers were on the scene at Heathrow.

Cullen didn't bother parking in the faculty lot where Elizabeth kept her car, but instead drove over the neatly kept lawn and cobblestone walkways to pull alongside several other police cars that had done the same.

"Wait here." He got out of the car and walked over to join the officers grouped in a semicircle around something lying on the ground.

It was the body, Elizabeth knew. The medical examiner was already on the scene and had undoubtedly pronounced death. Now it would be up to the officers and a crime-scene unit from the state police to gather evidence.

After a few moments, Cullen came back and got in the car. Elizabeth stared at him expectantly. "Well?"

"Same as before." He stared straight ahead. His features looked frozen, unnatural in the colored glare from the police flashers. "No blood on the body or on the ground."

Elizabeth shivered. "Her neck?"

"There's an incision. It's difficult to see out here, but I'm pretty sure we'll find needle marks on her arm, too." He paused and threw her an apologetic glance. "I hate like hell to ask you to do this, but I need you to take a look at the body. See if you can identify her."

Elizabeth nodded.

"You're okay with that?"

"I'm fine, Cullen. I know what has to be done."

They both got out of the car, and he slipped off his coat and wrapped it around her shoulders. As they walked toward the body, the group of officers parted and let them through.

The headlights on the police cars had been left on, and someone had set up a temporary light. Elizabeth stared down at the body. She recognized her at once. Waves of shock and nausea rolled through her. "I know her. She wasn't in any of my classes, but I've seen her around. She worked on the school paper. Her name was Morgan Hurley."

"You're positive?"

Elizabeth nodded.

"Any idea how to get in touch with her family?" Cullen asked.

"You'll have to get her address from Administration, but the office is closed for spring break. It won't be open until Monday."

"Does the guard have a key?"

Elizabeth hesitated. "I'm not sure, but I assume he has a key to all the buildings."

"What about the dorms?"

"I don't know."

"Private residences?"

She glanced up, startled. She'd never even thought of that. "No, I'm fairly certain he doesn't, but you'd have to ask him."

"I intend to," Cullen said grimly. "Just as soon as I find him."

Elizabeth's heart quickened. "George is missing? What if the killer—"

Cullen cut her off. "Let's not jump to conclusions, okay? Let's just stick to the facts." He glanced back down at the body. "You said after you'd climbed over the wall, you heard the gates open and a car drive through. But George wasn't in the guardhouse when you were there a few minutes earlier."

"No."

"So the suspect must have already been on campus."

"No, not necessarily. Curfew is at eleven, and George makes his rounds shortly after that. Someone could have come in then, and he wouldn't have seen them."

"How?" Cullen frowned. "Doesn't he have to let all visitors in through the gates?"

"The faculty are issued remotes so that we can come and go even when George is off duty or on rounds. Even the staff who live off campus have remotes."

Their gazes met for a moment, and Elizabeth knew they were thinking the same thing. The killer could be anyone, but the remote gave them a new lead. A new focus. As a member of the faculty, Paul Fortier had access to the campus. So did Lucian LeCroix. Elizabeth felt weak with fear, thinking of either man pursuing her through the darkness with evil in his heart.

"This doesn't necessarily mean someone who works at Heathrow is the killer," she said, trying to convince herself as much as Cullen. "With so many people away for spring break, someone could have broken into a car, stolen a remote, and it wouldn't be missed for days."

"That's possible." Cullen took her arm. "Come on. I'll walk you back to your house and you can pack a bag. You can't stay here tonight. It's not safe with everyone gone."

"What about George?"

"Yes, what about George?" Cullen said, his expression dark. "I have a feeling he's around here somewhere, lying low. Question is, why?"

AS THEY NEARED Elizabeth's house, she hesitated. The thought of the killer invading her private space, touching her personal things with death still on his hands made her physically ill. "I can't go in there, Cullen. Not yet."

He nodded. "No problem. I'll go in and throw a few things together for you. You okay with that?"

"Yes, thank you."

"You wait in the car.

A few moments later, they were headed back toward town. "I'll drop you off at your parents' house. You can spend the night there."

Elizabeth remembered the conversation she'd had earlier with her mother, and an uneasiness crept over her. She still couldn't understand why her mother had been so evasive, so secretive.

And why had she gone to Brussels so unexpectedly five years ago? Coincidence?

Elizabeth wanted desperately to believe that it was, but her mother's reticence was not exactly reassuring. Elizabeth didn't think she wanted to face her mother just yet. And besides, she didn't relish answering a lot of questions.

She tried to think of somewhere else she could go. To Kat's? That was no good. They weren't that close anymore, and besides, Kat owned her own private detective firm. Sometimes she had to work odd hours. If she was out on a case tonight, Elizabeth wouldn't want to alarm Kat's younger sister, Emily.

Brie? Unfortunately, she and Brie had lost touch as well. Actually, Brie had been the one to pull away, and Elizabeth had sometimes wondered if it was because Brie was afraid she and Kat would find out the identity of her child's father. As far as Elizabeth knew, Brie had kept the paternity a secret from everyone, and though Kat and Elizabeth had speculated about it plenty back then, they'd never been able to figure out who it was.

So Brie was out. Kat was out. And her closest friend at school, Rada Kilmeade, was off skiing in Vermont. Elizabeth turned to Cullen. "Just take me to the Moriah's Landing Inn."

He glanced at her nightgown. "Dressed like that? That should raise some eyebrows."

She shrugged. "I really don't care." Besides, she had no place else to go. But when Cullen passed downtown and headed toward the waterfront, she sat up. "You missed the turn."

"No, I didn't."

"Then where are we going?"

He kept his eyes on the road, staring straight ahead. "I'm taking you to my place. You'll be safe there."

His place?

Elizabeth sat back against the seat and digested this turn of events. He was taking her to his place? She was actually going to see where he lived? Maybe get some insight into his life?

Was this a new step in their relationship, or was Cullen simply being kind to her?

Elizabeth was still trembling by the time they reached his apartment building, but she thought it was as much from excitement as lingering fear. "You don't think my staying here will raise eyebrows?"

He shrugged as he led her up the stairs. "I really don't give a damn either."

But Elizabeth didn't think that was true. Not in the literal sense. She and Cullen both cared deeply what others thought. Why else had she hidden behind her aloofness and intelligence all these years? Why else had he turned bad as a teenager? Because they were both trying to pretend they didn't care when the fact was, they cared too much.

His apartment was on the third storey, and when he unlocked the door and stepped aside for her to enter, Elizabeth glanced around with great interest.

It was a small place with a living/dining/kitchen combination and a small hallway that led, she presumed, to the bathroom and bedroom. The area was clean and sparsely furnished, but the items he did have were nice—leather sofa and recliner, a new TV and sound system.

The main focal point, however, was the large bay window where, if she craned her neck far enough, Elizabeth thought she would be able to glimpse the sea. The window faced east, and she imagined glorious sunrises. Tonight, however, there was only a pale dusting of moonlight.

"Make yourself at home," Cullen said behind her. There was something in his voice, an odd, strained quality that Elizabeth had never heard before.

She turned from the window to face him. He'd moved back to the door after placing her bag on the sofa, and he watched her with a simmering intensity that caused Elizabeth's heart to skip a beat.

Then she realized the source of his fascination. Standing in front of the window, with moonlight drifting through the glass, the silky fabric of her nightgown must have been all but transparent.

She felt her face heat as her heart skipped another beat, then started to pound in overtime. "You're going back to Heathrow?"

"Yeah, but you'll be fine here. Lock the door after I leave. The bedroom's just through there." He nodded in the direction of the hallway. "Try to get some sleep. I don't know when I'll be back, so no sense waiting up for me."

Elizabeth swallowed. "All right."

He opened the door, but at the last minute, he turned back to face her. "By the way, while I was getting your things together, I found a book on the floor of your bedroom. I thought you might want it so I brought it along. It's in your bag."

Elizabeth caught her breath. Their gazes clung for an instant, and she could have sworn he smiled ever so slightly before he turned and left the apartment.

Face flaming, Elizabeth flew across the room and tore open the bag.

Nestled among a change of clothing and her toothbrush was a rare first edition of *Juliette's Diary: Her Secret Life,* Elizabeth's favorite volume of Victorian erotica.

TO HER SURPRISE, she was able to sleep after all. Locating a blanket, she curled up on the sofa so that she could hear Cullen when he came in. She dozed fitfully at first, but then, as the hours passed, she drifted into a deeper slumber.

When she awakened, dawn was breaking outside Cullen's window, and a gray light had settled over the room. Her first waking thought was that she was glad it was daylight finally, and her second thought was that she wasn't alone.

Gasping slightly, she sat up and looked around. Cullen stood at the window. He must have come in very late, and she hadn't heard a sound. The knowledge that she could sleep so soundly after a murder had just occurred was a bit unnerving.

He heard her stirring and glanced over his shoulder. "Morning."

Elizabeth stretched, then pulled the blanket up to her shoulders. It was chilly in the room. "When did you get home?"

"A little while ago." He looked as if he'd just stepped out of the shower and pulled on a pair of jeans. He was shirtless, and his hair was still damp.

"I didn't hear you come in," she said. "You could have been the murderer, for all I knew."

"I can be pretty stealthy when I want to be."

The better to slip from a woman's bedroom in the wee hours of morning, Elizabeth thought. "Why didn't you wake me up? I've been anxious to find out what happened."

He ran a hand through his damp hair. "There's not much I can tell you. The body will be autopsied later today, but I think we pretty much know what the findings will be."

"No sign of the killer?"

He shook his head.

"What about George? Did you find him? Is he all right?"

"Yeah, we found him."

Elizabeth's heart jumped at his tone. "Is he—"

"Oh, he's very much alive," Cullen said.

"Where was he?"

"In one of the dorms. With everyone away, he decided to use the opportunity to catch up on his sleep. Or so he says."

Elizabeth glanced up. "You don't believe him?"

Cullen shrugged. "He may have been in one of the dorms, but I doubt he was taking a nap."

"What do you mean—" Elizabeth broke off suddenly, remembering Kat's words the night George had caught them scaling the fence. *I wouldn't be surprised if he's planted a few hidden cameras in the dorms. Everybody knows the man's a perv.* She swallowed. "Do you think George could be the killer?"

Cullen hesitated. "Let's just say, I intend to keep a closer eye on him from now on."

Elizabeth glanced down at her hands, seeing them

tremble. Could she have been that wrong about George? She'd thought him harmless. Now she didn't know what to think. Who else might she be wrong about?

She gazed up at Cullen, watching the shadows across his face, glimpsing the darkness in his eyes. "You didn't find anything in the woods or in the cemetery?"

"No. But the fog made it damn near impossible to spot footprints or tire tracks. We'll go back out later once the sun burns off the mist and see if we can find anything, but I don't expect to. This guy doesn't seem to make mistakes. At least he hasn't so far."

"What about me?" Elizabeth asked softly. "I was able to get away from him. That was a mistake."

"Was it?"

His tone made her shiver. Elizabeth got up and wrapped the blanket around her shoulders as she walked over to the window to join him. "What do you mean?"

Cullen's expression turned grim. "There was no sign of a forced entry in your house. No evidence that he ever got inside. Maybe he wanted to make you think he'd gotten in so that you would run, so that he could pursue you. Maybe this is part of some sick game of his."

"But why me?" she asked a little desperately.

He shrugged. "Because he knows you're helping me on this case. And maybe you're the one person he's afraid will find him out." Cullen paused. "Think about it, Elizabeth. You're not only brilliant, you have a Ph.D. in criminology. The perfect foil for him. The perfect match."

Elizabeth clutched the blanket. "But why let me

go last night? If he's afraid I'll find him out, why not kill me when he had the chance?'' She stopped and glanced up at Cullen. ''Because he isn't finished, is he? The game isn't over.''

Cullen shook his head slowly. ''I don't think so.''

She closed her eyes briefly. ''This scares me, Cullen. Someone that cunning. That evil.''

He put his arms around her. ''We'll find him, Elizabeth. We'll stop him. I promise you that.''

''But when? Before he can kill again?''

He drew a weary breath. ''I don't know.''

They stood by the window for several minutes as the sun slowly rose over the sea. But it wasn't glorious as Elizabeth had imagined. It was the prelude of another day that the killer went free.

She lifted her face, and her gaze met Cullen's. There was something in his eyes…something dark and needy. Something that matched the urgency she felt inside herself.

He searched her face for a moment, and then seeing what he needed to, he kissed her.

HE LAID HER on the bed and placed one knee on either side of her. Then, planting his hands beside her head, he lowered his head to hers, kissing her again and again until Elizabeth thought she must have surely died and gone to heaven.

His body hovered over hers, barely skimming her, but everywhere they came into contact, her skin flamed from the intimacy, from the thrill of being so close. She lifted her hand and tentatively stroked his chest. He was so hard! His physique reminded her of those male models who did the designer underwear ads. Sculpted. Muscular. Intensely masculine. Looking at him was such a turn-on.

She grew bolder, running her hand up over his shoulders and down along his arms. Everywhere she touched was new male territory explored and conquered.

Returning her hand to his chest, she skimmed it downward, over his abs, and lower still, until she felt his stomach muscles contract and he drew a quick breath.

She snatched her hand away. That was close. A little too close.

Suddenly, she didn't know if she was ready for this.

He seemed to intuit her hesitation, and he broke the kiss to whisper his lips across her cheek, nuzzling her neck.

"Tell me something, Lizzie." His voice was husky against her ear. "What's a nice girl like you doing reading porn?"

She gasped. "It's not porn! It's literature. A classic!"

Cullen gave a low chuckle. "I saw those dirty pictures."

"I'll have you know those illustrations are fine works of art!"

"Right. And I read *Playboy* for the articles."

She realized then he was teasing her to help her relax, and she wanted to kiss him. He was so sweet and considerate, nothing like people thought him. "You read *Playboy?*"

"Uh, no. Just kidding." He ran his tongue around the shell of her ear, causing Elizabeth to shiver. "So tell me about that book."

She swallowed. "What do you want to know?"

"What's it about?"

"It's about...oh!" He was sliding his hand along her inner thigh, approaching dangerous territory himself. Elizabeth's stomach fluttered with nerves. With excitement. And more than a little apprehension. "It's about a young woman who travels to Victorian London to care for her maiden aunt. She has a series of...misadventures along her journey."

"Such as?" Now his hand was...and his fingers were...

Elizabeth's breath came in short, jerky little gasps. It took her a moment to answer him. "She...falls prey to...a mysterious stranger...who shares her coach...."

His lips nuzzled her neck. "What does he do to her?"

"He...kisses her."

"Like this?" He lifted his head to capture her mouth with his, coaxing open her lips, and then his tongue dipped inside, matching the rhythm of his fingers.

Elizabeth felt light-headed. On the verge of losing control. When Cullen finally broke the kiss, she whispered raggedly, "Exactly like that."

"What else does he do?" His eyes were dark slits of passion as he gazed down at her.

"He...undresses her."

A knowing smile tilted the corners of his mouth. "Like this?" Hooking his thumbs through the straps of her nightgown, he slowly slid the silk down her arms, and lower, until Elizabeth's breasts were completely exposed to his gaze.

Her first instinct was to cover herself, but when she reached for the quilt, Cullen's hand closed around her wrist. He bent and kissed her again, until Elizabeth's embarrassment began to melt away.

When his lips moved to her breasts, she squeezed her eyes closed, not wanting her natural shyness and inhibitions to dim the pleasure for even a moment.

He tasted her with his lips and then his tongue, and when she arched her back, he groaned, a deep, dark, sensual sound that sent a thrill of excitement coursing through her heated veins.

That he wanted her as much as she wanted him was an erotic thrill. A boost to her fragile ego that she desperately needed at that moment.

She plowed her fingers through his hair, holding him close to her breasts and thinking to herself, ''I always wanted my first time to be with you.''

He lifted his head. ''What?''

She went perfectly still. Surely she hadn't said the words aloud, had she? ''What, what?''

''What did you say?'' He'd pulled back, resting on his knees as he gazed down at her.

''I didn't say anything.''

''Yes, you did. You said you always wanted your first time to be with me.''

''So?'' She tried to shrug, but she was trembling too hard.

''So? This is your first time?''

He sounded almost angry. The heat of humiliation washed over her entire body. ''That can't come as much of a surprise,'' she whispered.

He let out a breath. ''Not entirely. I mean, I guess I knew. It's just…hearing it right before we were about to…''

''But it doesn't have to change anything,'' Elizabeth said, wishing she could crawl into a hole and never come back out.

"It changes everything." Sitting on the edge of the bed, he stared straight ahead. "Look, this isn't right. Your first time shouldn't be like this. You should have candles and romance and..." He rubbed the back of his neck. "Hell, I don't know. But I know it shouldn't be like this."

"Like what?"

"The aftermath of an adrenaline rush," he said bluntly.

That was all it had been for him? Elizabeth felt her own anger bubble to the surface. "You make it sound so...sordid."

"That's how you'd feel about it later, trust me."

"How do you know how I'd feel?"

He glanced at her. "Because I know you. You're not the type for a one-night stand."

Was that what this was going to be? He might as well have shot her through the heart with a dozen arrows. The searing pain couldn't have been more intense.

He sighed. "I told you before, I'm not ready for a serious relationship. I'm not ready to make a commitment to anyone. I'm still young, and you're even younger—"

Elizabeth sniffed. "Sounds like an excuse to me."

His features hardened. "Don't make this any harder than it already is."

She was supposed to make this easy for him?

She glared at him.

He lifted his hand in a helpless gesture. "I'm trying

to do the right thing here. I'm trying to be a man about this—''

"A man?" Elizabeth said coolly. "I'd say you're being more of a coward."

She couldn't have said anything that would have wounded him more. A shutter closed over his features as he got up from the bed and strode to the bathroom. "Sorry you feel that way," he muttered, before the door slammed shut between them.

IDIOT, IDIOT, IDIOT, Elizabeth scolded herself as she stood wrapped in her blanket, staring out the window in Cullen's living room. Why did she always have to say the wrong thing to him? Why not just accept his rejection and go peaceably on her way? At least a few scraps of pride might have remained intact, but no. She'd had to force a confrontation.

She heard him come out of the bedroom, and she glanced over her shoulder. He was fully dressed, on his way out.

"I'm going back to work," he said warily. "I don't know when I'll be home."

It doesn't matter, Elizabeth thought. *Because I won't be here.*

Not that she didn't want to be, but she couldn't face him now.

She nodded, then turned back to the window, not knowing what else to say to him. Actually, she did know, but why were the words *I'm sorry* so difficult to utter? Especially when one's pride was still stinging the way hers was.

She sensed Cullen's hesitation, as if he wanted to say something, too, but after a moment, she heard the door open and then close softly behind him.

So that was that, she thought, willing away the tears that stung behind her lids. Cullen Ryan had been an impossible fantasy, and maybe it was better she face that reality now and move on.

She was young. She had her whole life ahead of her. It was foolish to think that only one man could be her destiny.

"Destiny sucks," she muttered, wiping the back of her hand across the wetness on her face.

CULLEN PAUSED outside his apartment door, thinking maybe he should go back in and talk to her again, try to explain his reasoning, but knowing him, he'd just make things worse.

And besides, he really didn't think he could face the wounded look in her eyes that tore at his resolve. If he went back inside, he just might end up taking her to bed again, and this time, he wasn't certain he'd have the willpower to pull back.

For once in his life, he'd done the noble thing. He might not be the right kind of man for Elizabeth, but he was man enough not to take advantage of her when she was frightened and vulnerable. At least he could live with himself.

But he was afraid Elizabeth still didn't get it. Why they couldn't be together.

All she had to do was take a look around her, he thought grimly, glancing at the shabby facade of his apartment building. The cottage where she lived wasn't fancy, either, and he doubted she earned a huge salary from Heathrow College. But she lived within her means because she chose to. Cullen lived within his means because he had to. There was a big difference.

And supposing they did get together? For how long would she want someone like him accompanying her to fancy masquerade balls and stuffy gatherings at the college? How long before he became an embarrassment to her?

Cullen had his pride, if he didn't have much else, and he'd almost given that up in Boston. He'd gotten in with a bad crowd, and for a while, he was on the same downhill slide to the gutter as his old man. But somehow he'd picked himself up, shaken off the dirt, and turned his life around. Trying to live in Elizabeth's world just might send him straight back to that gutter.

With new resolve, he strode down the steps and headed out into his world, where a killer still roamed the streets.

Chapter Fourteen

If Cullen had avoided Elizabeth after their first kiss, he'd treated her as if she had the plague since that morning in his apartment. Weeks went by during which Elizabeth barely heard from him, and only then if there was some new information about the case to impart.

She tried to tell herself it was still possible he'd change his mind. He'd come around in time. And in the meantime, she still had the murder cases, as well as her classes, to keep her busy. She'd requested a copy of Morgan Hurley's autopsy report from Cullen to compare with Bethany Peters's, hoping that something would stand out to give them a clue. But other than the fact that the victims had shared the same blood type, she'd seen no similarities.

She had no doubt both girls had been killed by the same perpetrator. The incisions in their throats and the needle marks on their inner arms were almost identical. The fact that they'd both been students at Heathrow led Elizabeth to conclude that the school had to be the connection, although as far as she was able to determine, they hadn't even known each other. Bethany was a science major, and Morgan had been pursuing an arts degree. They didn't have the same classes, the same friends, nor did they live in the same dorm. Bethany was from Boston; Morgan was from a little town in upstate New York. Both were from privileged backgrounds, but so were most of the girls who attended Heathrow, except for a handful of scholarship students.

If the school *was* the connection, then that brought Elizabeth back to Paul Fortier. Bethany had been his student, but Morgan hadn't. Still, he could have seen her around campus, become attracted to her. Like Bethany, she was a very pretty girl, and Fortier seemed to have a penchant for beautiful women.

What is it they say? There is nothing quite so beautiful or poetic as a dead or dying woman.

There was another possibility, one that made Elizabeth shudder with dread. What if she, herself, was the connection? What if Cullen was right? What if the killer was trying to lure her into his sick game? What if he was taunting her with the bodies of students he'd chosen at random? What if the killings were about *her* and not the victims?

Elizabeth pulled her sweater tightly around her as she sat at her desk in her office. Tomorrow was Good Friday. The school was closed until the following Tuesday for the Easter holidays. The campus would be deserted as it had been on spring break. If the killer was going to strike again, she had a feeling it would be this weekend.

Since Morgan Hurley's body had been found, the school had hired additional security, but Elizabeth still didn't feel safe. She'd booked a room at the Moriah's Landing Inn for the weekend, and as she watched the exodus of students from the campus, she had a sudden urge to join them. She had no more classes for the day. What was keeping her there?

"Whoa, where's the fire?"

She'd vaulted from her office so quickly, she hadn't noticed that someone was standing in the hallway, just outside her door. Her heart started to pound before she recognized him. "Lucian! You startled me." She gave a shaky laugh.

"Sorry. It seems everyone around here is on edge these days."

"With good reason."

He glanced at her purse and briefcase. "Am I keeping you?"

"Actually, I was leaving for the day. I guess I'm anxious to start my holiday."

"Going somewhere special?"

She started to answer and then thought better of it. Maybe it would be best if she kept her plans to herself. "No, not really. I just want to relax a little."

"Well, you deserve it. You've had a harrowing semester, beginning that night at the Pierces' masquerade ball." His gaze deepened. "I can't help wondering if your discovery of both bodies is more than a coincidence, Elizabeth."

"How do you mean?"

A shadow moved in his eyes. "Just promise me you'll be careful."

"I will," but his warning lingered in her head even after she'd picked up her suitcase from her cottage and headed toward downtown. It was terrifying to think that she might somehow be the trigger for a madman's bloodlust.

Elizabeth wished desperately that she and Kat and Brie had remained close, so that she would have someone she could talk to about the murders, about her fears. But mostly she wished she had someone to confide in about Cullen.

Honestly, what was the matter with him anyway? He kept saying he wasn't the right man for her, but he was. He was! He thought she needed someone her intellectual equal, but he was the most interesting person she knew. And besides, just look at her parents. They were both brilliant, the perfect match, and they'd let their work consume them. They hardly spoke to each other these days, and Elizabeth suspected they no longer even shared the same bed. Did Cullen think she wanted that?

Or was he afraid he'd be like his mother, run out on his family when the going got tough? Or like his father, who'd turned to the bottle when he couldn't handle real life? Cullen was their son, but he was nothing like them. He wasn't going to become them any more than Elizabeth would turn out like her parents. It was true he'd flirted with the darker side of life before he'd left town, and she suspected in Boston as well, but he'd turned his life around, with no help from anyone. Look at the kind of man he was today. Good. Decent. Honorable.

Honorable to a fault, she thought dryly.

She drove past the turnoff to the inn and headed for the waterfront instead. She wondered what Cullen would do if she showed up unexpectedly at his apartment, but she was too much of a coward to find out. And the irony of that was not lost on her.

Instead, she parked on the street and walked slowly down Waterfront Avenue, past the tattoo parlor, the strip joints and Madame Fleury's, a fortune teller.

When she got to the end, she turned around and walked back.

Pausing outside the Beachway Diner, she wondered longingly if Brie was working this afternoon. She thought again how much she missed her old friends.

On impulse, she pushed open the door and walked inside.

BRIE WAS STANDING behind the counter, and when she saw Elizabeth, her expression grew wary. Then, a split second later, she smiled and motioned to an empty booth near the windows. Elizabeth nodded and walked over to sit down. After a few minutes, Brie came by with the coffeepot.

"It's been ages!" she said cheerfully. "How've you been, Elizabeth?"

"Well, considering I found two dead students in the last two months, not so good."

Brie gave her a sympathetic smile. "I heard about what happened. It must have been horrible."

Elizabeth nodded, her stomach going hollow at the memory of those bodies put on display. She couldn't help but believe the hanging was somehow symbolic. "It was bad, but I'm more worried about those girls' families."

"You always were strong," Brie said.

Elizabeth stared at her in surprise. "I…was?"

"I don't know who else could have gone through what you did in high school and come out so normal. All that teasing you had to endure just because you were younger and ten times smarter than everyone else. Kids can be so cruel, and all because your intelligence intimidated them. I always admired you for the way you handled yourself."

"You...did?"

Brie smiled. "You always did underestimate yourself, Elizabeth. I guess it's reassuring to know some things haven't changed." She poured Elizabeth a cup of coffee. "So what brings you to this part of town anyway?"

Elizabeth shrugged. "Would you believe, I happened to be in the neighborhood?"

Brie glanced at the clock on the wall. "Business is pretty slow. I can take a break in a few minutes if you'll hang around?"

"Sure." It was only two o'clock. Check-in at the inn wasn't for another hour. Until then, Elizabeth had absolutely no place to go or be.

But as if fate decided to take a hand in her plans, the door opened and Kat Ridgemont hurried inside. She waved to Brie, then glancing around, spotted Elizabeth and strode toward her.

Elizabeth had always marveled at the way heads turned when Kat walked by. She was tall and sleekly slender with long, black hair and dark eyes fringed with thick lashes. Dressed in a leather jacket over a T-shirt and jeans, she somehow managed to look tough and graceful at once.

"I thought I saw you walk by my office," she said. "I called out, but I guess you didn't hear me. You looked as if you were a million miles away."

"Sorry." Elizabeth motioned to the empty side of the booth. "Join me for a cup of coffee?"

Kat slid into the booth, folding her hands on the table as she leaned forward. "I've been meaning to call you. Cullen told me you're consulting on the investigation into these murders."

Elizabeth's gaze widened. "Cullen told you that? When?"

Kat shrugged. "The other day. I don't remember when exactly. We've helped each other out on cases from time to time, and we were talking…"

Her voice faded as Elizabeth suddenly became pre-occupied with an image of Kat and Cullen…together. It made her feel terrible because Kat was so much more Cullen's type than she would ever be. Elizabeth doubted he would have kicked someone as sexy as Kat out of his bed.

"…keep thinking about Claire," she was saying.

Elizabeth frowned. "What?"

Kat gave her a bemused look. "I said I can't help wondering if the killer is the same psycho who kidnapped poor Claire. If he's the same one who murdered my mother."

Any resentment that might have been building for Kat dissolved like mist in sunlight. "I've wondered the same thing myself," Elizabeth admitted.

"From what I understand, the MO isn't the same, though."

"Not altogether, no," Elizabeth said carefully. Even with a friend, she couldn't go spouting her mouth off about the cases. "But that doesn't necessarily mean anything. After twenty years, the killer could have changed his MO, either deliberately or through a natural evolution of his appetites."

Kat's gaze turned dark. "What if it *is* the same guy who kidnapped and tortured Claire? What if the killer's identity is locked up somewhere in her tormented mind?"

"Then she could be in danger," Elizabeth said. "But we've always known that. That's why her mother keeps her in Glen Oaks. The security is excellent.''

Brie came over then, and Kat slid over in the seat to make room for her. ''We were talking about Claire. And about the murders.''

Brie shuddered. ''Elizabeth and I were just saying what a horrible thing those girls' families are having to go through.''

''Yes,'' Kat agreed, her gaze clouding. ''Murder is horrible. And before another family is put through the same hell, I think the three of us should take a ride out to Glen Oaks and see Claire.''

''The last time I went, they wouldn't even let me in to see her,'' Elizabeth warned.

Kat nodded. ''I know, but they tell me she's getting better. Maybe if she sees the three of us, it'll trigger something for her. The last time we were all together was that night.''

''But Tasha was there, too,'' Brie reminded them sadly.

For a moment all three fell silent, caught up in the lingering grief over past tragedies, but then Kat shrugged off the melancholy. ''Look, I know it's a long shot, but I've always believed if Claire is ever going to remember, if she's ever going to open up to anyone, it'll be us. I say we give it a shot.'' Kat turned to Brie. ''Can you get away?''

Brie hesitated, then nodded. ''My shift ends in another hour. I like to spend all my free time with Nicole, but my mother is taking her to a birthday party down the street. I'll call and tell her I'll be late. I think you're right, Kat. We have to talk to Claire. At the very least, we owe it to her to try and help her get her life back.''

They clasped hands, and though their mission was a grim one, Elizabeth felt a camaraderie she hadn't experienced since that fateful night in St. John's Cemetery.

GLEN OAKS was a private institution located on the outskirts of a tiny village about a hundred miles west of Moriah's Landing. Safely tucked away behind an electronic fence which was artfully disguised by thick hedgerows of hawthorn, the white Colonial-style building was an elegant affair with a wide, sweeping drive lined with red oaks and sugar maples bursting with buds. Beds of winter crocus dotted the manicured lawn, and a stone fountain trickled near the entrance.

A nurse led them down an antiseptic hallway where the clatter of food trays could be heard through open doorways. "You girls came at an opportune time." She lowered her voice as she ushered them into Claire's room. "She's had a good day."

The room was decorated much like a young girl's bedroom, in pink satin and lace with mountains of stuffed animals on the bed. There was a vanity, but no mirror, and the glass in both the window and the door was doubled-paned and reinforced with wire mesh. Almost impossible to break.

Claire was seated in a rocking chair in front of the window, staring out across the sculpted lawn. She didn't turn when they came inside. She gave no indication whatsoever she was even aware of their presence.

She'd changed so much since that terrible night. She'd always been fragile-looking, with long, gorgeous hair and a pale, delicate complexion. But she was even more frail now. The cotton dress she wore hung like a sack from her lean frame, and her hair, though neat and clean, had lost its glorious luster.

Kat went over and knelt in front of her, placing her hand on Claire's knee. "Claire? It's Kat. Brie and Elizabeth are here, too."

Brie walked over and knelt beside Kat. "Hi, sweetie," she said in a soft, soothing tone, much like the one she undoubtedly used when she spoke to her little daughter. "What a pretty dress you have on!"

For the first time, Claire showed a slight reaction, a hint of emotion. She turned her beautiful blue gaze on Brie, and something that might have been a smile flickered across her features.

The nurse said to Elizabeth, "She loves to have her hair brushed. That might help relax her."

Elizabeth walked over to the vanity and picked up the brush, noting that the bristles were soft and pliant. Nothing that would cause any harm. She went to Claire and began stroking her hair, taking great care to be gentle.

After a moment, Claire's shoulders visibly relaxed. She still said nothing, but at least she wasn't screaming the way she had the last time Elizabeth had seen her. Elizabeth had heard those terrified shrieks all the way down the hallway, all the way home and sometimes in her sleep, she still heard them.

Tears smarted her eyes, but she willed them away.

Kat glanced up at Elizabeth, uncertainty flashing in her dark eyes. Elizabeth knew what she was thinking. How did they approach someone as fragile as Claire about what had happened that night? How, in good conscience, could they make her relive that nightmare?

Because it might save another young girl's life.

It might save Claire's own life.

Still, they would have to be very, very careful.

Claire reached a hand and touched Kat's cheek. Then she stroked one finger along Brie's curly red hair. "Pretty hair." She lifted a hand and felt her own limp strands. "I used to have pretty hair."

"Oh, honey, you still do," Brie whispered.

Elizabeth closed her eyes briefly. This was so much more difficult than she'd even thought.

"Claire, we want you to know something," Kat said. "We looked for you that night. We would have done anything to find you, to help you. We're so sorry we let you down."

"Hurt me," she whispered.

"Who?" Kat pressed gently. "Can you tell us who hurt you, Claire?"

"Hurt me again," she said more insistently.

"We won't let him hurt you again." Kat's dark eyes flashed with anger. "I promise you that."

"Hurt me." Then louder. "Hurt me! Hurt me! Hurt me!" A high keening emanated from Claire's lips, and Elizabeth stopped brushing her hair and stepped back. What had they done?

She remembered the awful guilt she'd felt that night when Claire had disappeared, how she'd been so certain it was all her fault because she'd been thinking about Cullen.

God help her, she was still thinking about Cullen while poor Claire—

She glanced up and saw him standing in the doorway.

It was as if her thoughts had conjured him from thin air. His gaze went from her to Claire, and a look came over his features that Elizabeth had never seen before. It was a combination of compassion, disbelief and a harder emotion that might have been determination.

"Get a nurse," Elizabeth said.

He turned, but before he could move, the nurse who had shown them in came bustling into the room. She went over and took Claire's arm, helping her out of the rocking chair. "There, there," she crooned. "It's okay. Everything's going to be okay."

She led Claire to her bed, and Claire lay down, curling herself into the fetal position while she clutched a pink bear to her chest. Her eyes were squeezed tightly closed as she rocked back and forth. The keening had stopped, but Elizabeth thought the silence that followed might even be worse.

"She needs her rest now," the nurse said briskly. "But I hope you'll come back again. It's good for her to have visitors."

"But she got so upset," Brie said worriedly.

"Yes, she did," the nurse agreed. "But any response is better than none at all."

Chapter Fifteen

It was late by the time they left Glen Oaks. Darkness had fallen in earnest, and as they exited the curving drive and pulled onto the main highway, Elizabeth could see a full moon rising over the treetops.

She rode with Cullen although she hadn't wanted to at first. She still felt awkward with him, but he'd made a point of asking her in front of Brie and Kat, and Elizabeth didn't think she could turn him down without arousing her friends' curiosity. If she'd insisted on riding back with them, they might have asked questions, and she didn't feel like talking tonight.

Earlier, she'd have given anything for someone to confide in, but now all she wanted was some peace and quiet to think about everything that had happened.

She stared silently out the window for the first several miles of the journey. If Cullen spoke to her, she answered in monosyllables. Finally he gave up and put in a Bauhaus CD. The dark, edgy music was the perfect accompaniment to her mood.

When they were almost home, he turned down the sound. "Okay, what's with the silent treatment?"

Elizabeth shrugged.

"Now you're just being childish," he accused. "You can at least answer me."

She turned to face him. "What do you want me to say?"

"Anything that's on your mind."

"My mind is a complete blank."

"You don't want to talk about your friend, Claire?"

"No." Which was true. The memory was still too raw.

"Do you want to talk about what happened in my apartment?"

"No!"

"I think we need to," he said softly.

"Well, I don't" Elizabeth folded her arms defensively. "What is there to say? You made your feelings perfectly clear, and for your information, now that I've had time to think about it, I agree with you. You're not the right man for me."

He threw her a startled glance. Then he frowned. "When did you come to that conclusion?"

"When you gave me no other choice." She turned back to the window. "I've been thinking about everything you said, and you're absolutely right. A woman like me needs candles and romance... whatever." She waved her hand absently. "My first time should be special, with a man who knows how to...you know. Someone older, perhaps, and sophisticated. Someone like...like...Lucian LeCroix." She slanted him a glance and saw his features harden.

"What the hell does *he* have to do with this?"

"He seems to fit the criteria you have in mind for

me. He and I are both college professors. We come from similar backgrounds. We have a lot in common.''

Cullen's voice hardened with anger. ''I told you before, I don't trust that guy.''

''But I do,'' she lied.

Cullen's gaze narrowed. ''You're just saying that to piss me off.''

''Am I?''

He turned back to watch the road, his face set in hard, furious lines. ''Mission accomplished.''

''I beg your pardon?''

''Nothing.''

Elizabeth lifted her chin. ''I'm just telling you what I thought you wanted to hear. You're off the hook now. You don't have to worry. I'm turning my attention elsewhere.''

''Like hell,'' she could have sworn she heard him mutter.

INSTEAD OF DROPPING her off at her car where she'd left it on Waterfront Avenue, Cullen headed south of town, turning on Old Mountain Road.

Elizabeth glanced at him in surprise. ''Where are we going?''

''To see David Bryson.''

''Why?''

''Emotions are running high around here. It's my duty to warn him about a dangerous situation that could be brewing.'' He shrugged. ''I wouldn't mind having a little chat with him about the murders, either.''

According to talk in town, David Bryson never left his house during daylight hours, but after dark, he prowled the streets, keeping to himself and to the shadows. Elizabeth had never personally spotted him, but she wondered sometimes if the occasional sightings of McFarland Leary couldn't be chalked up to Bryson's nocturnal wanderings.

Not that she didn't believe in ghosts. She was quite certain she'd seen one that night in St. John's Cemetery, but she wasn't about to confess her sighting to Cullen.

Old Mountain Road was a narrow, twisting trail that led, as its name implied, up the side of a mountain. At the top, clinging precariously to the edge of a jagged cliff, was the Bluffs, David Bryson's forbidden domain. As they neared the castle, Elizabeth thought that the stone facade blended almost seamlessly with the night.

There were no lights, save for a lone beacon in a tower window. A shadow moved across the light, and for a moment, Elizabeth could have sworn she saw someone staring down at them. She shivered, thinking of all the stories she'd heard about Bryson. A cold-blooded murderer. A horribly disfigured recluse. A man whose passions and grief could have driven him to do unspeakable evil.

Had they?

A butler—tall, rigid, impeccably dressed—opened the door. He was all set to turn them away, but then Elizabeth heard another voice in the background, and the man glanced over his shoulder. When he turned back, he opened the massive door and beckoned them inside. "This way."

The inside was even darker and more forbidding than the outside. The place was old and creaky, full of shadows and mysterious doorways. Elizabeth and

Cullen followed the butler down a long, dark hallway where he drew open a set of doors and waited for them to enter. Once they were inside, the doors closed with a resounding thud.

Elizabeth jumped a little, and goose bumps popped out on her skin. Judging by the crowded shelves of books, they were in a library of sorts, but the room was dank and musty, hardly inviting. The drapes at the window were drawn tightly, shutting out the moonlight, and only one lamp glowed dimly from a corner.

She and Cullen were both gazing around curiously. Elizabeth had assumed that David Bryson would join them momentarily, but as her gaze scanned the murky recesses of the room, she saw that he was already there. Either he'd been present all along, or he'd somehow slipped in from some secret passageway. She shivered as she felt his gaze meet hers.

"You've come about the murders." His voice was deep and velvety smooth. "I've been expecting you."

"I'm sure you have," Cullen said. "I've come by before, but your watchdog wouldn't let me in."

Elizabeth strained to see Bryson, but he'd positioned himself in deep shadow. Because of the scars?

"You'll have to forgive Richard. He's overly protective, I'm afraid, but then, he has good reason to be, considering that I'm the chief suspect in almost any criminal activity that occurs in this town." A hint of wryness crept into his rich voice.

"I know what it's like to be accused of something you didn't do," Cullen said. "I'm not here to make accusations."

"Then why are you here, Detective?"

"To warn you." Cullen paused. "Suspicions are

running high because of these murders. People are scared, and when they get scared, they're apt to do something stupid.''

''Are you saying the town's out to get me?''

''I'm saying if I were you, I'd hang close to home until all this blows over.''

Bryson's hand moved in a fatalistic gesture. ''I'm a recluse, Detective. Hadn't you heard? I never leave these castle walls.''

Elizabeth saw Cullen lift a brow slightly. ''Is that so? I've heard you like to take...long walks after dark.''

A polite way of putting it, Elizabeth thought.

''Is that a crime, Detective?''

''Not if walking is all you do. Any chance you were near Heathrow College on the night of March sixteenth?''

''As a matter of fact, I was.''

Elizabeth sensed Cullen's surprise. She turned to stare at Bryson, wishing again she could see his face.

''Were you on campus?''

''I didn't go inside the gates if that's what you mean.''

''What time was this?''

''Sometime before midnight. I can't be sure of the precise minute.''

Cullen and Elizabeth exchanged a glance. ''Did you see anyone enter or leave the campus either on foot or in a car?''

''I saw nothing.''

''What about the night of February fourteenth? Were you anywhere near the Pierce compound?''

''I was not.'' Impatience crept into Bryson's voice. ''I'm sorry, Detective, but I'm afraid I really can't help you out. I don't know anything about these murders. I can give you a piece of advice, though.''

"Let's hear it."

He leaned forward slightly, and for a split second, Elizabeth glimpsed his face. She caught her breath.

And then he stepped farther back into the shadows. "Check the victims' blood types, their medical histories. You may find something there."

"How do you know about their blood types?" Cullen asked sharply, but David Bryson had melted into the shadows.

Somehow he'd vanished without making a sound.

"HOW DID HE know that both victims had the same blood type?" Elizabeth mused as they made their way back down the mountains. "That information hasn't been released to the press."

"That's what I'd like to know," Cullen muttered.

"And what did he mean about their medical histories?"

"I've been wondering that myself." Cullen lifted his hand to rub the back of his neck. "But when he said that, I felt as if I should know what he was talking about. Like maybe there's something I've forgotten or haven't connected yet. You know how it is when you can't quite put your finger on what it is that's bothering you?" He snapped his fingers suddenly. "Wait a minute. I think I *do* know. When I first interviewed Bethany Peters's mother, she kept wringing her hands and crying over and over that Bethany had always been the picture of health. She'd never been sick a day in her life. How could something like this happen to her?"

"I'm sure it was just a figure of speech," Elizabeth said. "She was very upset."

"Maybe. But she was pretty adamant. And one of Morgan Hurley's friends said something along those lines about her. She was never sick. Might be worth taking a look at their medical records and see if we can find other similarities."

To what end? Elizabeth was about to ask, but then she turned to Cullen as something occurred to her. "Remember the test tube we found in the cooler room with Bethany's body? What if someone who knew Bethany's blood type and her medical history wanted to get a sample of her blood for some reason? An experiment, maybe?"

"But the cause of death was exsanguination. Her blood was drained. The killer would have known that."

"It's almost impossible to drain a body completely of blood," Elizabeth pointed out. "But I'm not talking about the killer. I'm suggesting someone other than the killer may have wanted a sample of Bethany's DNA. If we could find out who all knew about those blood types and medical histories and why they were so significant, then we might be able to figure out why someone wanted those girls dead."

"We already know that Bryson knew." Cullen frowned. "It still seems a long shot to me. Although…" He trailed off into thought.

"What?"

"I was just thinking about something Shamus McManus said to me once. We were in the Beachway Diner, and it was right before I was called to the Pierce compound after you'd found Bethany's body. He said that McFarland Leary rises every five years to come searching for the 'offspring of his offspring,' I think is the way he put it."

"What did he mean by that?"

Cullen shrugged. "I'm not even sure he knew what he meant. Marley Glasglow was there at the time, and he warned Shamus about sticking his nose where it doesn't belong. I'm thinking Shamus may have overheard something he wasn't supposed to."

"Like what?"

"I don't know. But Shamus also asked me if I ever wondered why so many scientific types settle in Moriah's Landing. I think that's starting to sound like a damn good question."

"Oh, I don't think there's any mystery to that," Elizabeth said. "There are a lot of major universities in the area, and Boston is a fairly easy commute. Plus, the Pierce Foundation awards a lot of grants. It could be simply a case of following the money."

"Maybe. But I've been asking some questions around town about Leland Manning ever since we saw him that night. He has a laboratory right there on his property. If he has the background and credentials you say he has, why isn't he affiliated with some Ivy League university, or some hotshot private research institution? And what about his weird theory on witches? If anyone is conducting bizarre experiments, I'd put my money on him. And another thing." He glanced at Elizabeth. "He's not the recluse that David Bryson is. He frequents a bar down on the waterfront."

"Manning?" Elizabeth had a hard time picturing the rather formal man they'd met the other night in a waterfront bar.

"That could be where Shamus overheard something he shouldn't have."

"But that still doesn't tell us what he heard," Elizabeth mused. "Or if it's connected in any way to the murders." She sighed, rubbing her temples with her fingertips. "It's all giving me a headache, just talking about it. Two months and two bodies, and we're still no closer to finding the killer. Face it, Cullen. He could be anyone. Bethany had a class under Paul Fortier, and it's possible something more may have been going on between them. But Morgan was an arts major. She wasn't required to take biology. Then there's Leland Manning. Yes, he lives fairly close to the campus. Yes, he has a laboratory on his property. And, yes, he has some pretty strange theories. But where is the connection to the victims? Same with David Bryson. He was a suspect in the murders twenty years ago, but nothing was proven then, and we don't have anything on him now except that he somehow knew, or at least guessed, that Bethany and Morgan had the same blood type and maybe similar medical histories. So where does that leave us?"

"You forgot to mention your friend, Professor LeCroix. As freshmen, wouldn't both girls have been required to take an English class?"

Elizabeth waved an impatient hand. "Yes, but Bethany was dead before Lucian ever arrived in town."

"Assuming he arrived when he said he did."

"Yes..."

"You're still defending him, I see." Cullen gripped the wheel as the car shot around a sharp curve. "Still figuring on him being your first lover?"

Elizabeth gave an embarrassed laugh. "I know I

implied that, but I was just…hurt. A little angry, I guess.''

"You must have had some thoughts in that direction or you never would have said anything."

"I haven't. I don't know why I said anything about him." She gave him a pleading look. "Can we just stick to the investigation right now? If you have something on Lucian LeCroix, let me hear it."

Cullen glared at the road. "His credentials checked out."

"You ran a background check on him?"

He shrugged.

They both fell silent, both deep in thought, and then, as they were nearing the cemetery, Cullen said, "I keep thinking about Claire."

Elizabeth turned. "I know. It's still a shock to see her like that. She was always so beautiful and the most gentle person I ever knew. That something so horrible could have happened to her, of all people."

"Vanished without a trace," Cullen muttered.

"What?"

He tapped his fingers on the steering wheel. "How the hell did someone get her out of that mausoleum without any of you seeing anything?"

Elizabeth felt the old familiar rush of guilt. "You don't know how many times I've asked myself that same question."

He was slowing the car, and Elizabeth glanced around. St. John's Cemetery was to their left, and Cullen pulled off the road near the gates.

"What are you doing?" she asked in alarm.

"I'm going to have a look around."

"Why?"

"Because there has to be some way that she was taken from that crypt."

"But the police searched it. They didn't find anything." Elizabeth knew her voice sounded slightly desperate, but she couldn't help it. The last time she'd been in that cemetery, she'd been running for her life.

"Yeah, but I know the guys on the force," Cullen said dryly. "Most of them won't even walk under a ladder. It's my guess they gave the mausoleum a cursory search, at best."

Elizabeth stared at the cemetery gates, a terrible dread welling inside her. "You don't expect me to go with you, I hope."

"As a matter of fact, I do." Cullen's eyes gleamed in the darkness. "I need you to show me exactly where you and the others were when Claire disappeared."

"This can't wait until morning?"

His expression turned grim. "Another girl could be dead by morning."

He was right. If there was a clue inside that mausoleum that could stop the killings, then Elizabeth wasn't going to let a little fear stand in her way. Cullen reached over and removed the gun from the glove box.

"I'm leaving the safety on this time, but if we run into trouble..." He showed her how to flick it off. "Like I said before, just point and shoot."

Easier said than done, Elizabeth thought. Her hands would be shaking so badly she would be lucky not to shoot Cullen. Or herself.

He checked his own weapon, then returned it to his shoulder holster. He glanced at Elizabeth. "Ready?"

"No."

He grinned. "It'll be okay. We'll stick together. I won't let you out of my sight."

"Promise?"

"You got it."

THE CEMETERY looked different tonight. No storm clouds threatening on the horizon. No fog creeping through the landscape. Just a pale, fragile moon casting a mysterious glow over the tombstones and mausoleums. A mild breeze stirred shadows, making the city of the dead seem almost…alive.

Topping a low hill, Elizabeth paused, her stomach clenching in fear. "That's it." She pointed to a crypt directly ahead of them. "I can tell by the broken cross. Leary's grave is somewhere to the right of it."

"Show me."

Elizabeth took the lead, uncertain that she would be able to find Leary's grave in the dark, but she moved unerringly to it, staring down at the headstone worn smooth by time and weather. "This is it. This is where we were. We formed a circle around the grave. Then we drew lots and Claire lost. She got up and walked to the mausoleum alone."

"Show me."

Her heart pounding, Elizabeth crossed the ten yards or so to the crypt, taking some comfort in the knowledge that Cullen was right behind her and they were both armed, although she still had her doubts about her ability to shoot anything. Besides, how did one kill a ghost?

Cullen reached around and tried the door of the crypt. It opened easily, and Elizabeth remembered how Kat had had to struggle with it that night. Had someone been here recently?

"You can wait out here if you want to," Cullen told her. "I'll leave the door open."

Elizabeth glanced over her shoulder, her gaze scanning the headstones as she remembered how the fog had formed into a human shape over Leary's grave. The manifestation had probably been a combination of an active imagination and intense fear, but Elizabeth didn't relish a repeat performance.

"That's okay," she said, suppressing a shudder. "I'll go in with you."

The crypt was a fairly large one, and old, with a thick carpet of grime covering the marble floor and cobwebs draped from the ornate ceiling. The place smelled of death and decay, but then Elizabeth wondered if that was her imagination, too.

Cullen played his flashlight over the walls. "I don't see another door. How the hell did he get her out of here?"

He shone the beam along the wall vaults. They were stacked on top of one another, and each contained a stone plaque. Elizabeth read some of the epitaphs. Beloved Wife and Mother. Our Dearest Son.

An angel holding a lantern had been carved into the stone on one of the bottom vaults and the inscription read: An Angel Walks Among Us. Follow Her Light to His Sanctuary.

"Wait," Elizabeth said, when Cullen moved the light to the next vault. "Go back."

She knelt and ran her hands over the angel.

"What is it?" Cullen asked.

Excitement spiraled through Elizabeth. "Do you remember all those old newspaper clippings I have hanging on the walls in my house? I've always been an avid history buff, especially about anything pertaining to Moriah's Landing. I have hundreds of books in my collection, and I like to go to flea markets whenever I can—"

"Elizabeth," Cullen said impatiently. "Get to the point."

"Moriah's Landing is famous—or infamous, depending on one's perspective—because of the witch executions in the 1600s, just like Salem. But both towns were also active in the Underground Railroad before the Civil War. The symbol of a safe house was a lantern hanging from a hitching post. But there are no hitching posts in cemeteries."

Cullen knelt. "You think this place was used as a station in the Underground Railroad?"

"Read the script," Elizabeth told him. "'Follow Her Light to His Sanctuary.' A sanctuary is a haven. A safe place. That could also explain how the rumors got started about the mausoleum being haunted. The conductor, whoever he was, wanted to scare people away."

Cullen looked doubtful. "It's hard to imagine runaways hiding in here. Someone could have easily stumbled upon them, in spite of the rumors."

"I don't think they hid in here," Elizabeth said, waving an arm to encompass the crypt. "I think they hid in here." She tapped the vault. "My guess is there's a series of catacombs or tunnels beneath the mausoleum. They might even lead all the way to the sea, where a ship would take the runaway slaves to freedom."

"I guess there's only one way to find out."

The openings to the vaults were hinged, so that coffins could be slipped into place, and then the doors were closed, sometimes sealed.

A small metal handle had been set into the stone at the bottom, and Cullen gave it a tug. When it didn't budge, he laid aside the flashlight and used both hands. The door gave a little, then finally creaked all the way open.

Cullen picked up the flashlight and angled the beam inside. The vault was empty.

He gave her a tight smile. "Nice work, Sherlock. Now we know how Claire's abductor was able to drag her off right under your noses."

He leaned forward, thrusting the upper part of his body into the vault. "I can see steps." His voice echoed in the abyss. "Looks like they lead down to some sort of cellar. If you're right, there should be an opening to a tunnel somewhere down there."

He started to crawl into the vault, but Elizabeth grabbed his leg. "What do you think you're doing?"

He glanced over his shoulder. "I'm going to have a look around the cellar. See if I can spot the opening to the tunnel."

"Cullen! Are you crazy? That cellar has been there for over a hundred and fifty years. It could cave in at any moment."

But he was almost all the way into the vault by now. Elizabeth had to lean inside to see him. He was at the stairs. Going down.

"Cullen!"

"I'll be right back. Wait for me up there." He took something out of his pocket and tossed it to her. Miraculously, Elizabeth caught it. It was his cell phone. "If anything happens, call the station. Get some help over here."

Elizabeth backed out of the vault and sat on her heels. Without the flashlight, the crypt was very dark.

She could feel something crawling on her neck, and then she realized it was goose bumps. She was chilled all over, and it came to her in a flash the reason for her terror.

She was no longer alone in the crypt.

Her heart began to beat in long, painful strokes. Someone, *something* was right behind her, but she didn't dare turn around. She didn't want to see Leary's ghost....

A flesh-and-blood arm grabbed her by the throat and pulled her to her feet. Elizabeth struggled. She tried to cry out. But it was too late. She heard the phone clatter to the floor just as a cloth was shoved against her mouth and nose.

A split second before the ether overcame her, she saw a foot kick the vault door shut, trapping Cullen inside.

Chapter Sixteen

Cullen heard the vault door slam and rushed back up the stairs. "Elizabeth! Open the door!" But he realized almost at once that she would never have closed that door on purpose. Someone must have come into the vault.

The killer...

"Elizabeth!" Cullen shoved against the door until he worked up a sweat, but after several moments, he realized he was having a hard time breathing. The effort was using up all the oxygen in the cellar.

He turned and surveyed his options. *Option*, he amended. There was only one thing he could do. Find the opening to the tunnel and follow it out.

And then it hit him. The full extent of his predicament.

He was trapped underground....

In a small, close space....

No air...

Panic rushed up from his stomach, into his lungs, pressing against his chest. He couldn't breathe....

Get a grip, a voice commanded him. Elizabeth was in dire trouble. He didn't have time to go all mental.

He hadn't had a problem entering the vault, so why was he panicking now?

Because he was trapped, that's why.

Cullen didn't know when or why or how he'd developed claustrophobia, but he thought it might have been when his mother left. After she'd taken off, he'd sometimes awakened in his small cell-like room, gasping for breath, drenched in sweat.

He felt that same helplessness now, but he fought it. He had to get out of there. Elizabeth was in big, big trouble.

The thought of her calmed him somewhat, and he played the beam of his flashlight along the walls of the cellar. To his right, a small opening, barely large enough to accommodate a man lying flat on his stomach, led, perhaps, to freedom.

But could he do that? Could he force himself into such a narrow space? Even for Elizabeth?

An image came to him suddenly. He could see Elizabeth lying on a table, her features pale and fragile as the blood was slowly drained from her body....

A new panic seized him then, and he strode across the tunnel, dropping to his knees in front of the opening. He could do this. To save Elizabeth, he would do anything.

He slithered into the tunnel, clutching the flashlight, putting one hand in front of the other as he inched forward. He forced himself to think about how Claire had been dragged along that same tunnel. How terrified she must have been. All these years, she'd lived in her own private hell, and now it was up to Cullen to find her kidnapper, to finally bring him to justice.

And so he made himself keep going.

After long, agonizing moments, the tunnel widened and he was able to stand upright. That was better. Not much...but better....

He walked along, feeling spiders crawl in his hair and along his back, but he knew that was just the panic. After a while, the air in the tunnel began to smell fresher, and he thought he could hear the distant sound of the ocean. His first instinct was to run toward the sound, but caution held him back.

The tunnel, as it turned out, had melded into a cave, the mouth of which opened in the side of a cliff. Thirty feet below him, the surf pounded against the rocky shoreline, but tonight there was no boat waiting to take him to freedom, no beacon of welcome or warning except for the distant shimmer from the lighthouse.

Cullen glanced up. It was another twenty feet or so to the top, and from there a long hike down Old Mountain Road to the cemetery where he'd left his car. But that seemed his best shot. He started to climb.

He was almost at the top, ready to reach a hand over the edge of the cliff and pull himself up when he happened to glance up. A dark form dressed in dark clothing stood at the top of the cliff, staring down at him.

David Bryson...

WHEN ELIZABETH came to, she was lying on her back on a stainless-steel table. She could feel the smooth, cool surface beneath her bare skin, and that's when she realized she was naked.

Naked!

Where was she? She blinked, trying to focus, but all she could see were vague shapes. She struggled to sit up, but a wave of nausea rolled over her, and groaning, she collapsed against the table. Which was just as well, seeing as how she was strapped down.

Strapped down!

She glanced around frantically as everything came back in a horrifying rush. The mausoleum. Cullen! He was trapped underground! His claustrophobia! She had to get to him!

Elizabeth redoubled her efforts to sit up, but it was no use. She fell back, gazing frantically around. *Where was she?*

There was a picture on the wall beside the table, and she concentrated until it came into focus. It was an anatomical chart representing the circulatory and muscle systems of the human body.

Was she in some sort of classroom? A science lab?

She moved her gaze to the closed door just to her right. There were danger signs mounted on the white surface, a warning that this was a formaldehyde area.

Elizabeth's heart started to beat painfully. At the end of the table on which she lay were a series of hoses and pumps. A shelf above her head contained several bottles of fluid in different colors. Some of them were pink. Embalming fluid…

She gasped in horror. She was at the funeral home. In the embalming room…

A scream bubbled in her throat, but Elizabeth forced it back. She couldn't panic. She had to find a way to free herself. And then she had to go and rescue Cullen.

She closed her eyes, trying to think what to do. When she opened them again, a man in a white lab coat stood over her.

"You're awake, I see."

Elizabeth blinked. He wasn't at all who she'd expected to see. "Lucian?" He looked like Lucian and yet he didn't. His eyes were different. No longer dark, but a piercing blue. She'd seen those eyes before....

His smiled broadened. "Allow me to introduce myself, Elizabeth. I'm Dr. René Rathfastar."

Rathfastar? Manning's protégé?

"I'm also known as Lucas Cross, the fisherman who rents the apartment above Krauter's Funeral Home. I'm sure you've figured out by now where you are."

She moistened her lips, trying to will away her fear. "I thought René Rathfastar was dead."

"As you can see, I'm not."

"You killed those girls?" When he merely kept smiling, she said almost accusingly, "But that day in the lab. The sight of blood made you sick."

He sighed. "An affliction I've never gotten over, I'm afraid. It stems from my childhood, when my father, who was an avid big-game hunter, made me dress his kills. It's ironic, I suppose, that that which repulses me also...stimulates me."

Elizabeth swallowed. "Why did you kill them?"

"You would have figured that out eventually. That's one of the things I admire most about you. Your fine mind. We have that in common, you know. I was a prodigy, also, and I know how lonely that can be. I was drawn to you...for many reasons."

The thought of that made Elizabeth even more ill. She tried to calm her racing heart. She had to keep her wits about her so she could figure out his motive. So she could get one step ahead of him.

"I don't understand why you're doing this." She

let an edge of panic creep into her voice. He would like that.

"Oh, I think you do understand. You were on the right track, you just didn't realize it. But one day soon you would have had an epiphany, and then everything would have fallen into place for you. As much as I hated to bring our little game to an end, I couldn't let that happen. I couldn't let you ruin my plans. I've waited so long."

"Since Brussels?" She took a stab in the dark at his motivation.

His gaze hardened. "Since Leland Manning forced me out of the society. And in the process, he ruined my reputation, my career. He took everything from me. I had to flee the country, to try and start over in Europe, but even there, he still had influence. He still pursued me. Then *I* had an epiphany."

"What was it?" Elizabeth struggled unobtrusively with the bindings that kept her trapped on the table. Bindings that Rathfastar had attached himself because an embalming table usually had no need of them. Elizabeth's thoughts were slightly hysterical, but she couldn't seem to rein them in.

"The car accident was the catalyst," he said. "I'll spare you the details of the hell I went through, the months in the hospital, the dozens of agonizing surgeries I had to endure. Suffice it to say, I survived. And I came through the ordeal a new man." He smiled again. "Literally. I look nothing like my former self, but..." He stroked his chin. "I can't say that I'm displeased with the results."

"What about the real Lucian LeCroix?" Elizabeth thought she already knew the answer.

"Dead," he said flatly. "I knew him in college,

you see. When our paths crossed again in Europe, he didn't recognize me. I used an alias to strike up a friendship with him, a bit like that movie. You know. *The Talented Dr. Rathfastar.*" He laughed, pleased with himself. "Anyway, LeCroix told me about a relationship he'd been in that had gone sour. He was nursing a broken heart and needed a change of scenery. An old friend of his mentor's, a friend LeCroix himself had never actually met, had gotten him a position at Heathrow College. It was, quite simply, fate. The perfect way to return to Moriah's Landing. The perfect chance to ruin Leland Manning as he ruined me."

"How?" Elizabeth wriggled her hand. If she could somehow manage to slip it free—

"This is beneath you, Elizabeth."

"What?"

"I can see right through you, you know. You're not going to be able to get away. Not this time. Let's just get on with it, shall we?" He turned, picking up a syringe from the tray of instruments behind him.

"Wait!" Elizabeth cried.

He glanced down, needle poised over her arm. "This won't hurt much. Just a little sample for my own purposes, and then we'll get to the really serious bloodletting." He reached a gloved hand out and stroked her throat.

Elizabeth's skin went clammy with terror. "If I can't escape, why not tell me what I want to know? It's not like I can hurt you with the knowledge." She stared up at him, her eyes pleading. "How could killing those two girls ruin Manning? He's not even a serious suspect."

"He will be. Think about it, Elizabeth. The matching blood type. The similar medical histories. The test tube you found in the funeral home. All that was carefully planned. Everything will eventually lead to Manning, a scientist working with DNA. People already wonder about him and his strange theories. Each new kill will bring the police closer and closer to his door."

"Each new kill?" Elizabeth whispered. Dear God, how many did he have planned?

He saw her face and shrugged. "Oh, come now. You didn't think I was finished just because *our* little game has reached its conclusion, did you?"

She shuddered.

"In fact, Manning's next victim lay right where you are less that twenty-four hours ago. Her blood has already been flushed down the drain, and now she's on ice, if you'll pardon my bluntness, at my place on Raven's Cove, waiting for the right time to…make her appearance. But don't worry, Elizabeth. I'll spare you her identity. Why have that on your conscience in the last seconds of your life?"

Oh, God, who had been his third victim? Brie? Kat? Claire? Terror rushed through Elizabeth's veins so fast and so furious she could hardly think straight. Hardly keep from screaming, but she knew she had to somehow stay sane. Rathfastar was brilliant, but so was she. She could find a way to outsmart him….

"How did you know I was getting close to the truth?" she asked softly.

He cocked his head. "Your cop boyfriend was starting to ask questions around town about Manning. That's what I wanted. But you. You were asking questions about *me*. About the society. Sooner or later you would have figured it all out."

"But…" How had he known she'd asked questions about the secret society? She hadn't talked to anyone except her mother….

And then she remembered Marion's evasiveness. Her unwillingness to talk about Manning and Rathfastar. Elizabeth recalled her mother's sudden trip to Brussels, where Rathfastar was last seen, where he'd had a terrible car accident….

She gazed up into his eyes. Those eyes that were no longer brown, but blue, fringed with thick lashes.

She had seen those eyes before. And now she knew where.

An image of her little brother formed in her mind. His sweet face. His light blue eyes. His features that were not like either of his parents' or his sister's, but unique.

Now she knew why.

"You…and my mother?" she whispered in horror.

He might have looked wistful if not for those eyes. There was nothing behind them. "My brilliant and beautiful Marion. You think she told me of your interest in the society? I wish I could still count on her loyalty, but she made her choice a long time ago, I'm afraid." He shrugged. "As it happens, I've managed to cultivate a new friendship in the police department. She was—shall we say?—persuaded to copy Detective Ryan's case files for me. He keeps copious notes, by the way. Unusual for someone of his limited talents. You would be shamefully wasted on someone like him, Elizabeth."

The taunt hardly registered. Her mind was still on Brandon. It couldn't be true. *Please don't let it be true.*

"It is interesting that you should bring up your

mother, though.'' He glanced down at Elizabeth, his gaze skimming her nude body. ''You're so much like her.'' He ran the tip of the syringe along the inside of Elizabeth's arm, teasing her. ''When I'm long gone from here, when Leland Manning has become only a shell of his former self, then I'll find a way to let Marion know that I was the one who killed her daughter. That's the price she'll pay for her betrayal. And as for the boy…''

A wave of fresh terror swept over Elizabeth.

''You're wondering the same thing that's tormented me for years, aren't you, Elizabeth? Is Brandon my son, or isn't he?''

While they'd been talking, Elizabeth had managed to work one hand free of the straps. When Rathfastar turned to adjust the embalming pump, she glanced around frantically for a weapon.

The only thing she could see were the bottles of liquid on the shelf near the table. She reached up and grabbed one, working frantically to uncap the lid with one hand.

When Rathfastar turned back around, she flung the liquid into his eyes. He screamed, lifting his hands to his face, bending double in pain.

Then his hands dropped, and he was laughing. ''It'll take more than a bottle of distilled water to thwart my plans, Elizabeth.''

He reached for a scalpel from the tray of instruments. ''You've got a little more fight left in you than I anticipated,'' he said admiringly. ''Perhaps we should do something about all that energy.''

Elizabeth bit back a scream. That was exactly what he wanted, to see her terrified.

Somewhere behind her, Elizabeth heard a door burst open, and Cullen shouted, "Rathfastar!"

He looked up, surprised.

"Put it down," Cullen yelled. Elizabeth couldn't see him, but she could hear what sounded like the clomp of running feet through the receiving area. He'd brought reinforcements.

Rathfastar hesitated, surprised to have his plans interrupted. Especially by someone with such limited talents.

Elizabeth could have wept in relief. But only for a moment.

Rathfastar turned back to her, the scalpel poised over her throat. "Perhaps it is you who should drop your weapon, Detective. One slice, and she's through."

A shot rang out, catching Rathfastar in the shoulder. Stunned, he staggered back a few steps, still clinging to the scalpel. A look of rage came over his features, and he lunged toward Elizabeth.

Cullen fired again, and this time the bullet hit Rathfaster in the chest. The scalpel fell from his fingers as his legs folded and he collapsed to the floor.

Cullen ran across the room and loosened the straps, and Elizabeth sat up, clinging to him. He took off his coat and wrapped it around her. "How did you know?" she asked breathlessly. "How did you know where to find me?"

He hesitated. "I guess we'll have to chalk it up to intuition."

"You don't believe in intuition."

"Then maybe I also got a little help from an unexpected source."

"What source?"

"I'll tell you all about it later. Let's get out of here. This place gives me the creeps."

Outside the funeral home, Elizabeth turned to him as she clutched his coat tightly around her. "I was so worried about you. The thought of you in that awful place. Trapped with your claustrophobia..." She lifted her hand to his face. "I was trying to get free so I could come and rescue you."

He swore under his breath, and then he drew her into his arms and held her so tightly she could hardly breathe.

Chapter Seventeen

Elizabeth came out of the dressing room and stood in front of the mirror. She hardly recognized herself. The dress she wore was…revealing, to say the least. Black. Short. Clingy.

She tugged at the low neckline. "I don't know about this."

"It's what you asked for," Becca Smith reminded her.

"Oh, I know. You did a beautiful job. It's just…"

"It's just *hot,* is what it is." Kat lounged in a chair near the mirror, eyeing Elizabeth with new respect. "That should bring Cullen up…er…around nicely."

Elizabeth glanced at her coolly. "I'm sure I don't know what you mean."

Kat laughed. "Oh, come on. You've wanted to jump his bones for years. Admit it."

Elizabeth's cheeks turned bright pink.

"You should see your face," Kat teased. "It's like an open book. You never could keep a secret. You'd better leave the subterfuge to Brie."

Elizabeth thought of Brandon and the possibility that a vicious killer was his father. That was one secret she would take to her grave.

Kat got up and sauntered to the door. "I have to get back to the office, but let me know how that dress works out for you. I may want to borrow it. I thought I might try one of those online dating services, see what's up with that." She opened the door, then turned back. "Oh, a piece of good news. I heard from Claire's mother this morning. We've all been feeling so badly for upsetting her when we went to see her, but turns out, she started getting better after that. She may even get to come home for a visit."

Elizabeth gazed at Kat in alarm. Would that be safe?

Kat shrugged, intuiting her look. "If she does come home, we'll have to watch out for her," she murmured.

Elizabeth was still thinking about Claire when she left Threads a few minutes later. Whoever had kidnapped and tortured Claire was still out there. Leslie Ridgemont's murderer was still out there, too, but at least Rathfastar had been stopped. His latest victim, Dana Colby, had been found, as he'd claimed, in a cooler in the house he'd rented on Raven's Cove. She, too, had been a student at Heathrow, and Elizabeth's heart went out to her family.

It would take a long time for the town to get over this latest reign of terror. As for Elizabeth, she planned to keep working on the mystery of the matching blood types and the similarities in the victims' medical histories in hopes that her research would lead her to the original killer. And to Claire's kidnapper. There were still too many unanswered questions in this town, and Elizabeth wouldn't rest until she found out the truth.

But for now…first things first.

She slowly climbed the steps to Cullen's apartment. Taking a deep breath, she knocked on his door.

When he answered, he looked as if he'd just come from the shower. He wore jeans and a shirt buttoned up only part of the way. When he saw her, his brows lifted in surprise. "What are you doing here?"

Elizabeth knew she looked different. She wore a trench coat over the dress, but even so, she'd left her hair down and she had on makeup. "May I come in?"

He stepped back so she could enter. Elizabeth's legs were shaking so badly she hoped she didn't topple off her stiletto heels.

She turned.

Cullen's gaze was all over her. "What's going on?"

"I just came by to see how you're doing. I haven't seen much of you since we wrapped up the case." He'd gone back to avoiding her, but Elizabeth wasn't about to stand for it this time. Not without a fight. She fanned her face. "It's warm in here, isn't it. Mind if I take off my coat?" She let it slide down her arms.

Cullen's eyes almost popped out of their sockets when he saw the dress.

Slowly, she walked toward him.

He backed away from her, until he was up against the wall. "What are you doing, Elizabeth?"

"Can't you tell?" she asked in a sultry voice she'd been practicing for days. She ran the tip of her finger down his partially-revealed chest. "I'm trying to seduce you."

He caught her hand. "Well, stop it."

Elizabeth froze. If she'd been humiliated before, she was positively mortified now. Why had she ever thought she could pull this off? What was she doing here anyway? Couldn't she take a hint?

She started to pull back, but Cullen clutched her hand. "I told you once that your first time should be special. With the right guy."

Elizabeth swallowed. *But I've been in love with you forever,* she wanted to tell him. Some remnant of pride, thank goodness, held her back.

"This isn't the right time, Elizabeth."

"I'm finally starting to get that message." Her feelings for him were hopeless.

"I'm not sure you are, so let me spell it out for you." One arm crept around her waist. Slowly, he drew her toward him. "The next time I carry you into my bedroom, you'll have a ring on your finger that says your mine forever. Got it?"

Elizabeth stared up at him, stunned. "But you said...the way you've been avoiding me...I thought..."

"I've been avoiding you because I needed time to think. When I saw you on that table at the funeral home...when I thought about what could have happened to you..." He closed his eyes briefly. "It was like I'd been struck by lightning. I couldn't believe I hadn't seen it before."

"Seen what?" Elizabeth asked in a trembly voice.

"How much you mean to me." He gazed down at her. "No one's ever looked at me the way you do, Elizabeth. No one's ever cared about me before. I guess I was too scared to believe it could be real. That it could last."

"But it is real," she said. "I've loved you for a very long time, Cullen. That's never going to change."

His gaze turned tender. "It took almost losing you for me to come to my senses. For me to see what was right there in front of me. You're an amazing woman, Elizabeth."

"How come it took you so long to figure that out?" she teased. "It's been days since you rescued me."

He swallowed. "I know. But even after I realized how much…how I felt about you, I was still scared, I guess."

"Scared of what?"

He shrugged. "This isn't going to be easy. Let's not kid ourselves."

Unease fluttered inside Elizabeth. "What do you mean?"

He drew a long breath and released it. "I'm not like you. I'm not from your world. I'm a cop. A high-school dropout. The son of the town drunk." He waved a hand. "Take a look around you, Elizabeth. This is who I am."

"I know who you are, Cullen. I've always known. I may come from a privileged background, but you can't imagine how lonely my life has been without you. I may have a high IQ, but you're the smartest, most interesting person I've ever known. And as for my parents—" She shuddered. "They have their faults, just like yours did. But it's who we are that matters. It's what we've made of our lives. Don't you see that?"

He smiled. "I'm beginning to."

"Then why can't you say it?"

"Say what?"

"That you love me."

He wove his hands through her hair, tilting her face to his. "I love you, Elizabeth. I'm crazy about you.

You're the most beautiful woman I've ever known. I've never wanted anything in my life as much as I want you at this moment.''

"Oh, wow," Elizabeth whispered, and then she said nothing else because Cullen bent at that moment and kissed her. Tenderly at first, and then fiercely. With the promise of a passion that took her breath away.

"About that book you were reading..." Cullen murmured into her ear. "Where were we...?"

And the story continues...
Next month don't miss
the next installment of

MORIAH'S LANDING:
HOWLING IN THE DARKNESS

By B.J. Daniels

Chapter One

A killer fog rolled in off the Atlantic, moving silently through the darkness as it approached the small town nestled at the edge of the sea.

Jonah Ries didn't see the fog coming any more than he could see the future. But he felt it. At first, just a disquieting sense of foreboding. Then he came roaring up over a rise in the rocky landscape and saw the sign: Welcome to Moriah's Landing, and he knew, a soul-deep knowing, that this was the last place on earth he should be.

He slowed his motorcycle, the feeling so strong he actually saw himself flipping a U-turn in the middle of the road, throttling up the bike, his taillight growing dimmer and dimmer beneath the twisted dark limbs snaking over the pavement.

But he could no more turn back than he could convince himself he had nothing to fear in Moriah's Landing. He knew what he would risk coming here. A hell of a lot more than just his life, he thought, as he swept down the hill, past St. John's Cemetery without looking in that direction, and headed for the wharf.

He felt the first hint of the fog long before he saw

it. Small patches of dampness brushed past his face, ghostlike as spiderwebs. But the moment he turned down Waterfront Avenue, the thick mist moved in, as solid as wet concrete, obliterating everything, forcing him to pull over, park his bike and walk the rest of the way.

Might as well just get it over with. He reached under the left side of his leather jacket for the reassuring feel of his .38 nestled in the shoulder holster. Snug as a bug. Too bad what he feared most couldn't be killed with a bullet. Not even a silver one.

He made his way along the brick sidewalk toward the faint beat of the neon bar sign at the end of the street, unable to throw off the ominous feeling he'd gotten at just the sight of the town's sign.

Nor had he realized how late it was until he saw that the shops were dark, locked up for the night. Of course it wasn't Memorial Day yet. That's when the tiny Massachusetts town would come alive with tourists, especially this year, with Moriah's Landing celebrating its 350th anniversary.

Tourists would flock here for the beach—and the witch folklore, bringing a morbid fascination for the town's dark, witch-hanging past.

Tonight though, the small township lay cloaked in a fog of obscurity, silent as McFarland Leary's grave, as if waiting for something to happen. Unfortunately, Jonah knew what that something was.

"Hey!" A voice came out of the fog and darkness at the end of the street near the blurred, flashing sign for the Wharf Rat bar. Jonah could barely make out the form, but instantly recognized it, just as the man coming out of the bar had recognized him. "Hey."

The man staggered forward, then stopped, clearly shaken momentarily from his drunken state.

Jonah reached blindly for the first door next to him, grabbed the handle and turned, praying it wouldn't be locked, but prepared to use whatever it took to get in. He shoved with his shoulder as he turned the handle, losing his balance in surprise as the door fell open and he stumbled in, closing it behind him.

"You're late," a female voice admonished.

He froze, his back to the dark room. From beyond it, a narrow path of light ran across the carpet to his feet. He turned slowly, comforted by the feel of the .38 against his ribs.

She stood behind a large antique desk, one hand on her hip, her head cocked to one side so her long mane of raven's-wing-black hair hung down past her shoulder like a wave. He could feel her gaze, dark and searching, long before he stepped close enough to really see her face.

"Sorry," he said, without thinking. He had plenty to be sorry about so he didn't mind.

Her eyes narrowed. "I guess you didn't get my last e-mail."

He shook his head and looked apologetic. Unfortunately, he hadn't gotten any of her e-mails.

"Are you ready?" she asked, sounding a little unsure of herself. He sensed this was new territory for her and wondered what a woman like her was doing going on blind dates, if that's what this was.

Ready? He watched her pick up her purse and jacket and then hesitate. He couldn't help but stare at her. She had the most interesting face he'd ever seen. Wide-set summer-blue eyes with dense lashes, a full, almost pouty mouth and high cheekbones, all put together in a way that startled and interested him at the same time.

"Yes?" she asked, eyeing him, definitely not sure now. "Is there a problem?"

Not unless being totally confused was a problem. He started to tell her that she was making a mistake. But then she came around the corner of the desk and he got the full effect of her little black dress.

Wow. It was a knock-out dress on her against the warm olive glow of her skin. Silver glittered on her wrist, dangled from the lobes of her ears and swept the curve of her neck and throat. Nestled in the hollow between her breasts hung a small silver lighthouse charm.

"Did you have some spot in mind?" she asked. The tap of her heels drew his attention back up to her face as she moved toward him.

He had lots of spots in mind. But she'd caught him on a night when he was already off-kilter and she was the last thing he'd expected to run across. So it took him longer than it should have to realize she thought he was her date—an online blind date, it seemed. Even worse. And from the way she was dressed, they were going out for a drink? Maybe a late supper?

Unfortunately, her "real" date would probably be along any minute. Jonah realized he'd be damned disappointed when that happened.

This Mother's Day Give Your Mom A Royal Treat

Win a fabulous one-week vacation in Puerto Rico for you and your mother at the luxurious Inter-Continental San Juan Resort & Casino. The prize includes round trip airfare for two, breakfast daily and a mother and daughter day of beauty at the beachfront hotel's spa.

INTER·CONTINENTAL
San Juan
RESORT & CASINO

Here's all you have to do:

Tell us in 100 words or less how your mother helped with the romance in your life. It may be a story about your engagement, wedding or those boyfriends when you were a teenager or any other romantic advice from your mother. The entry will be judged based on its originality, emotionally compelling nature and sincerity.
See official rules on following page.

Send your entry to:
Mother's Day Contest

In Canada
P.O. Box 637
Fort Erie, Ontario
L2A 5X3

In U.S.A.
P.O. Box 9076
3010 Walden Ave.
Buffalo, NY
14269-9076

Or enter online at www.eHarlequin.com

All entries must be postmarked by April 1, 2002.
Winner will be announced May 1, 2002. Contest open to
Canadian and U.S. residents who are 18 years of age and older.
No purchase necessary to enter. Void where prohibited.

PRROY

Creaking floorboards...
the whistling wind...an enigmatic man
and only the light of the moon....

*This February Harlequin Intrigue revises
the greatest romantic suspense tradition of all
in a new four-book series!*

Moriah's Landing
A Modern Gothic

Join your favorite authors as they recapture the
romance and rapture of the classic gothic fantasy in
modern-day stories set in the picturesque New England
town of Moriah's Landing, where evil looms but
love conquers the darkness.

#650 SECRET SANCTUARY by Amanda Stevens
February 2002

#654 HOWLING IN THE DARKNESS by B.J. Daniels
March 2002

#658 SCARLET VOWS by Dani Sinclair
April 2002

#662 BEHIND THE VEIL by Joanna Wayne
May 2002

from

HARLEQUIN®
INTRIGUE®

HARLEQUIN®
Makes any time special ®

*Available at your
favorite retail outlet.*

Visit us at www.eHarlequin.com   HIML